Olympian

Heartbreak

Other Works by Andrya Bailey

Olympian Passion
Olympian Love Trilogy, Book 1

"No Inhibition"
featured in *Waves of Passion*

Olympian Heartbreak

Olympian Love Trilogy

Book 2

Andrya Bailey

To everyone who makes

the ultimate sacrifice for love.

Believe.

To my loving parents.

And to the reason for everything

—H.

Contents

Acknowledgments

With sincere and deep appreciation for:

Konstantinos Karatolios, a talented teacher, historian (Byzantinologist), social anthropologist, and author, for providing historical accuracy with his invaluable insight into and expertise on Greece's history, mythology, and current facts.

Edward M. Wolfe, an amazing author and beta reader extraordinaire, for his priceless feedback and editing suggestions.

Daniela Owergoor, the professional digital and book cover artist who was so patient and creative in coming up with the concept for and designing the beautiful cover.

The muse who is inspiring me to create this trilogy.

The awesome readers, without whom this story would not be alive.

All who motivated, supported, and offered me suggestions and feedback during the production of this book.

One

THE BUZZ OF THE phone startled me. I woke up experiencing a temporary lack of awareness of time, space, and reality, having fallen asleep with my clothes on and with the cell phone clutched in my hand. I was tired, and my emotions were drained. The phone kept buzzing. The room was dark, so I pressed the talk button without checking the number. My hello came as a whisper.

"Sabrina, did I wake you up? Were you able to sleep? I'm five minutes away from your place. I'm coming over to take you to breakfast before we go to work." Jane's voice rushed through like a tornado. Processing her questions took me a few seconds. "Are you there? Are you okay?" she persisted in the absence of my response.

"Hi, Jane. I was sleeping."

"Sorry. I know it's early. But I can't stop thinking about you. How are you feeling about Nikos going to Greece all of a sudden? I want to make sure you're okay before getting to the museum today. I'm about to turn into your apartment's parking lot."

"Come on up then. But I'm fine. I just need to take a shower and get dressed. And thank you for coming," I said before hanging up.

A few minutes later, I opened the door to find Jane frowning at me.

"I knew you weren't fine. You fell asleep with your clothes on. Did you cry yourself to sleep?" she asked, giving me a hug.

"I miss him so much, Jane. I can't believe he's gone." I led her into the living room and closed the door.

"Have you heard from him at all?" Jane made herself comfortable on the couch.

"Sort of . . . I think. He sent me a text. It's actually . . . a song."

"A song? He sent you a song?"

"Here. You can listen to it, then tell me what you think after I get out of the shower. I don't want to hear it again or I'll be in tears."

I showed her my cell phone; the screen shone with the link to the song Nikos had sent me. It was the only message I had gotten from him after he left Houston without saying goodbye. I walked back to my bedroom and closed the door behind me, for I didn't want to listen to that song again. Just thinking about Nikos was enough for my eyes to fill up with tears. Going to the museum today would be difficult. I was ready for this internship to be over so I could go back to school and finish my master's degree. And stop thinking about my summer romance.

As if forgetting Nikos would be that easy.

I undressed and stepped into the bathtub, letting the hot water from the shower caress my face. The image of Nikos stripping naked and getting into the bath with me the first night we made love was vivid in my mind. Tears flowed in a stream, mingling with the steamy water while I sobbed. I had to be strong; after all, I had known all along Nikos had come to Houston for only two months on his museum assignment and would go back to Greece afterward. Maybe it was better for me that he'd left so hastily. With no goodbye, no drama, and no empty promises, I'd be forced to get over him sooner.

I had to mend my broken pieces. Numbness still enveloped my senses, but when I finally came out of the shower, I felt better. My tears had dried. Jane was still sitting on the couch holding my phone, and when she saw me coming, she frowned and pressed the mute button.

"What?" I asked.

"This is just . . . I'm not sure how to describe it. For real. He leaves the country in a rush, and all he can do is send you a sad song? Are you serious?" She shook her head, staring at the phone with a quizzical expression.

I walked toward her, took the phone back, and saved Nikos's message.

"Do you think he sent me the song because he didn't know what to tell me?" I sat on the loveseat next to her.

"Yeah, it's possible." Jane scratched her head. "I'm not saying it's not romantic. In fact, this is one of the most romantic and touching things I've ever seen a guy do. But he should have called you to say goodbye instead of hiding his feelings behind a song's lyrics. Too much drama . . ."

I nodded. "There's nothing he could've said for me to feel better, though. Maybe it was easier for him. You don't like him much, do you?"

She rolled her eyes at me. "It's not that I don't like him. I don't like what he does or did to you. I'm still not convinced there is nothing between him and Maggie. The whole thing is bizarre. I hope you get over him soon. The internship is about to end, and you won't have to go to the museum daily, at least for a while."

"True," I said, "but forgetting him will be hard, regardless. Anything Greek I see in the museum and anywhere in the city will remind me of him. I'm in love with him, Jane; you know that. More than I thought possible. I can't stop thinking about him."

"You need a boyfriend to forget about Nikos. What about giving poor Steve a second chance? I heard he hasn't been dating anyone since you guys broke up. I believe he still likes you . . ."

I got up from the loveseat and walked up to the window, gazing idly at the manicured lawn of the apartment complex. "Jane, please. I appreciate your concern, but I need time to heal. I can't think of being with anyone else right now. Nikos is the man I've always dreamed of. I'll never find anyone else like him. It was love, lust—whatever you want to call it—at first sight. It was mutual. Nikos wanted me. Maybe it was just a physical thing, but our chemistry was undeniable. Rarely do you find someone with whom you click so much in all aspects. He's a dream. My dream. And now I'm awake to the nightmare of not having him." My eyes filled with tears, and I knew I was going to have a meltdown if we didn't stop talking about Nikos.

Jane got up from the couch and came toward me, holding her car keys.

"Let's go to breakfast. And we're not going to talk about Nikos."

She drove to IHOP, and even though I had no appetite, she insisted I eat something. I ended up ordering coffee and a hefty plate of scrambled eggs, hash browns, and pancakes. We tried not to talk about Nikos, and Jane did a fabulous job changing subjects whenever his name came up. I knew she was trying hard to keep me afloat; otherwise, I would be diving headlong into a major depression.

When we got to the museum, I took a deep breath before getting out of Jane's car. I had a hard time registering the fact that I wouldn't see Nikos. I looked around the parking lot, searching for his rented car.

"He's gone, Sabrina. Gone. Forget him. Come on. We need to go to work." Jane touched me lightly on the arm, nudging me toward the museum's entrance.

I shook my head. She was right, but I was not ready to give up my feelings for him. We entered the museum in silence after agreeing to go to lunch together. I was glad I wasn't working in the Antiquities department, where Nikos had spent his time there. No one would talk about him in the Arts of Africa, Oceania, and the Americas, where I had been placed for my internship. I'd be able to finish my project there without hearing his name. I had to stay as far away as possible from the Greek vases exhibit Nikos had been responsible for if I were to remain sane during these last couple weeks of the internship.

When Jane texted me to remind me about lunch, I declined. The big breakfast still sat in my stomach, and I just wanted to stay in the gallery working. The last thing I wanted was to be around people who knew Nikos. Jane understood and left me alone. By five, we were ready to go home.

"How was your day?" Jane started the car and backed out of the museum's parking lot.

"It was actually better than I thought. If I occupy myself with work, I have less time to think about him." I stared out the window while we waited for the light to turn green. "I wasn't in the mood to see anyone, you know."

"Yes, I get it, girlfriend."

Jane turned on the AC, and a blast of cold air blew on my face.

"Did anyone mention anything about Nikos?" I asked.

"You mean Curt?"

I pushed the AC vent away from my face. "Yeah . . . Curt. If anyone would find out anything about Nikos, it would be Curt, right? He was the lucky one, working with Nikos in the Antiquities department."

Jane chuckled. "No, Curt didn't say anything. He asked how you were doing, and I said that under the circumstances, you were fine."

"Jane, I do appreciate all you're doing for me. You're such a great friend. Thanks for helping me cope."

"That's what friends are for, right? Anyhow, take it easy and call me if you need anything." She was soon parking in front of my apartment building.

"Thank you. I'll see you tomorrow, then."

I hopped out of her car and waved goodbye as she slowly backed up and drove away. I walked unhurriedly to the building and climbed the steps to my apartment on the second floor, but as soon as I stepped inside, my mood deteriorated. I looked around as if lost, not knowing what to do, what to think, or how to react. How long would I hurt like this? It was an empty feeling, a vacuum, a huge space full of nothing inside of me. Suffering from Nikos's absence was more overwhelming than I thought possible.

I dropped my purse on the couch and wandered toward my bedroom. I had to occupy myself before this absurd feeling destroyed me. Pacing back and forth, I heard the cell phone buzzing. I picked it up and checked the display, but it was an unknown number, so I dismissed it. It buzzed again a second later. The unknown caller insisted. Being in no mood to talk to telemarketers, I dismissed it once more. And again, it buzzed a few seconds later. Determined to put an end to the insistent and annoying unknown call, I pressed the talk button.

"Hello. This number is in the National Do Not Call registry. Please remove it from your list. I don't appreciate receiving calls from unknown numbers." I vented my frustration at the caller.

"Sabrina?"

The exotic accent made my hands sweaty. I sat down on my bed; my heart pounded loudly with the realization Nikos was calling me.

"Nikos? I'm sorry, I thought it was . . . an unknown caller; I thought the telemarketers . . . and . . ." I had no idea what I was saying. I mumbled as if I were having a nervous breakdown. I had to calm myself.

"How are you?" he asked, interrupting my babbling.

My breath caught in my throat. I wanted to cry out to him. *Oh, Nikos, I miss you so much!* I was at a loss for words. I wanted to be in his arms. "I'm fine, I . . . I'm glad to hear your voice. What happened?" I held the phone as close to my ear as possible. I wanted to hear Nikos's every breath.

"I'm sure you're confused and upset with me. I must know how you're doing. I've been thinking about you the whole time since I left."

I stared blankly at the walls. "I was appalled when I found out you'd left. I . . . I saw you coming into the museum with Maggie that morning. And then you were gone."

"Remember when I told you the Mycenaean jewels from the National Archaeological Museum were going to be loaned to a private collector? See, they were stolen while they were being prepared for the transfer. The only reason I went to the museum that morning was to alert Dr. Jones I had to get back to Athens immediately."

I grabbed a pillow and hugged it tight. "Why did you leave without saying goodbye?"

"I'm sorry. It all happened too fast." He cleared his throat. "Did you get my text?"

"The link to the song?" I whispered.

His breathing grew heavy. "Yes."

"What did you mean when you sent me the song?" I shut my eyes tight with apprehension. I wanted him to tell me how much he missed me.

"I wasn't sure how to break the news to you. I had planned on spending that night with you. But Mr. Wallendorf wanted me in Athens as soon as possible to handle the situation, and he flew me over in his private plane," he said. "It was an emergency."

I set the pillow back on the bed and laid my head down on it. "I miss you, Nikos. I'm so disappointed. I never thought you'd leave in a hurry . . . without saying goodbye. You didn't even leave me a note. I'm not sure what to think."

"Sabrina." He cleared his throat again. "I didn't want to say goodbye. I don't want to say goodbye. I want to see you again. I need to go back to Houston, but I'm busy taking care of this mess now."

"You're coming back?" I asked to confirm what I thought I heard him say.

"I have to. I need to be there in person for negotiations with the museum and the Greek vases exhibit. I wasn't planning on leaving so soon while I still have pending business to attend to. But most importantly, I want to see you."

A sigh of relief escaped from my mouth. It was all I needed to hear to get strong and endure his absence. There was hope after all. He wanted to come back and see me again. "Oh, Nikos, I was afraid I'd never see or hear from you again." I rolled around on the bed and kicked my heels up in the air.

"I didn't leave you, Sabrina. I couldn't do that to you."

I switched the phone to my other ear. "What happened to the jewels? Will you be back after they're found?"

"Unfortunately, I can't tell when I'll be back quite yet. The situation here is . . . complicated."

I sat up and placed the pillow on my lap. "How complicated?"

He gave a deep sigh before answering, as if he hesitated to talk about it. I pictured him pacing around. He might be combing his fingers through his hair as he usually did when he was upset or anxious.

"It's not only the jewels. It's . . . it's my family, too. My brother's been missing for the last few days, and my mother has no idea of his whereabouts. It's not the first time he's left, so I'm hoping he will return soon. But I'm glad I'm here. She needs me."

"I'm so sorry to hear that. I'm sure your mom is very worried. But I hope everything's okay with your brother and he gets back soon."

"I hope so, too. I don't want to be delayed here because of him. But I need to make sure my mom calms down." His voice was raspy, and he sounded worried. "Anyhow, I need to be here until the situation with the jewels is under control so Maggie can go back."

"What about Maggie?" I'd been so happy to hear from him I'd forgotten Maggie had gone to Greece with him. Just the mention of her name was enough to send me into an insanely jealous mode. Nikos had told me her father had sponsored the loan of the jewels to one of his friends, a British art collector. He had also assured me there was nothing going on between them. But I couldn't help it. Maggie had told me over and over she was his girlfriend whenever she had a chance. I threw the pillow back on the bed and bit my lower lip.

"Maggie is here representing her father. She will go back to Houston within the next few days. There isn't much for her to do here. She can't help with the investigation or anything much, actually. She's not a museum employee, and she can't speak Greek. Her presence is but a formality."

My jealousy didn't subside. I took a deep breath, but my heart still raced. "Is she staying with you?"

"Of course not. She's in a hotel. I'm not with her. Don't you trust me?"

I nodded in silence, although I knew he couldn't see me.

"I don't want you to be upset, Sabrina. I'm thinking about you, and I want to see you as soon as I can." His voice sounded reassuring.

I rested my head back on the pillow. "I do, too . . . I miss you, Nikos. It's hard to believe you're not here. The museum is not the same without you." *I'm not the same without you.*

"We'll figure something out. I'll keep you abreast of what is going on around here. Keep up with your work and your research. And call me if you need anything from me."

I need you. Here with me. Now. Call you if I need anything from you? All I need is you . . . Oh, Nikos. I want you more than anything. I want to be with you.

"Yes, I will," I said instead of repeating my thoughts.

"I have to go now. It's two in the morning here, and I need to get some rest. I'm sorry I left without saying goodbye. I want you to know I can't get you out of my mind, Sabrina. Have a good night. I will call you."

The line went dead. Nikos was gone. I stared at the phone as if in a trance. I still couldn't believe I had talked to him, yet he was so far from me. It had been such a relief to hear his voice. I would be able to function better. There was hope. He wanted to see me again and had plans to come back to Houston.

But Maggie was still there with him.

Two

"WHAT HAPPENED? YOU LOOK different. No, not different. Happy. Definitely not somber," Jane said as we sat down for lunch.

I had gone to the museum's cafeteria, where I knew I'd find her, along with Curt and Robert. Having my favorite college buddies working in the museum's summer internship program with me had been so much fun. I loved hanging out with them. And after talking to Nikos the night before, my attitude about his departure had changed. There was no reason for me to be so gloomy.

"Infused with energy, I should say." Curt's beautiful blue eyes blinked at me while he gave me a playful smile.

"Nikos called me last night." I took a sip of my water and pretended to be busy with my ham and cheese sandwich, avoiding their stares.

"You don't say!" Robert exclaimed, tapping me lightly on the leg.

Jane gasped. "He called you?"

I nodded.

"So? Is he coming back?" Jane's arms waved frantically.

I put the water bottle down. "He's planning on coming back, but he has to stay there for now to help out with an investigation. Some Mycenaean jewels were stolen from the museum where he works, and that's why he had to go back in a hurry." I tried not to get too personal about the conversation I'd had with my Greek god.

"What about *dear* Maggie? Why did she go to Greece with him?" Curt grabbed a piece of bread and spread butter on it.

My face heated up when I heard Maggie's name. I rested my elbows on the table. "It seems her presence there is a mere formality. She's representing her father. Mr. Wallendorf sponsored the loan of the jewels; apparently he invested money in the transaction. But according to Nikos, there's nothing she can do to help."

"What a mess! I'm sure we'll hear all about it when she comes back. Dr. Jones is having a hard time canceling Nikos's previously scheduled engagements and lectures. There's no one to replace him on such short notice. It's a shame." Curt shook his head.

"So, tell us. Hearing Nikos on the phone was enough to infuse you with so much energy, as Curt said?" Jane asked.

I smirked. "It was good to hear his voice and find out how he's doing. But I wish he was here."

"Hello, there. May I please interrupt your lunch for a moment?" Dr. Jones, dressed impeccably in a light-brown suit, suddenly appeared next to us. He was carrying a bottle of iced tea and a take-out bag. The museum's restaurant was busy, and we hadn't noticed him approaching our table.

"Hi, Dr. Jones. Yes, please, would you care to sit with us?" Curt motioned to an empty seat next to him, inviting Dr. Jones to sit down.

Dr. Jones shook his head. "Thank you, Curt, but I have a conference call in a few minutes. Could you please stop by my office after lunch?"

Curt's eyes widened. "Is something wrong?" He sounded worried.

"No, no, nothing to worry about." Dr. Jones turned to me. "And you too, Sabrina, please. I'm looking forward to seeing you both."

I nodded. "Yes, sure, Dr. Jones. We'll be at your office shortly."

"Enjoy the rest of your lunch. Now if you'll excuse me, I need to run." He was gone in the blink of an eye and left us all staring at each other.

11

Jane broke the silence. "Why would he want to talk to both of you? Do you think it has anything to do with Nikos?"

"I have no idea," Curt answered. "Now I'm dying of curiosity and can't even finish my food." He took a sip of his water and pushed his plate away.

Jane leaned on her chair, chewing on her lips. "You guys better tell me what he wants as soon as you find out."

Robert slapped Curt's arm. "I hope it will be good news about the work you've been doing."

"We'll find out soon enough." Curt rubbed his hands together in excitement. He finished his water and used a paper napkin to dry his mouth.

When we were ready, Curt and I walked to Dr. Jones's office. Roxanne, his administrative assistant, was at her desk and greeted us when she saw us coming.

"Hello, there. Dr. Jones asked me to welcome you into his office. He'll be back in five minutes," she said, showing us to Dr. Jones's spacious office.

She invited us to sit down on the chairs facing his desk and offered us something to drink. Since we'd finished lunch not long before, we politely refused, so Roxanne went back to her desk.

We sat in silence, admiring the beautiful artwork decorating the walls. Two pastels by Mary Cassatt caught my attention. The soothing colors of the paintings had a calming effect that eased my apprehension.

"Hello, Curt. Hello, Sabrina." Dr. Jones entered the office, startling me. Before we had a chance to respond, he continued. "I'm glad you stopped by. I've been busy with Dr. Soulis's unforeseen departure, as you can imagine. And there's been one thing after another since." He took his place on the chair behind the desk and stared at us for a few seconds before continuing. "Would you be available to go to Greece in three weeks?"

The question came as unexpectedly as a heavy blow to my head. I stared at Dr. Jones, speechless. Did he just ask if we were available to go to Greece in three weeks? The question seemed to have had the same impact on Curt, because I didn't hear a whisper from him.

"I can see you are both stunned by my question," Dr. Jones said. "I'm sorry I just blurted it out without explaining. Allow me to elaborate." He opened a drawer in his desk, removed a small piece of cleaning cloth, took his eyeglasses off, and rubbed the lenses with it. "Every year, at the end of the summer, the museum offers its members an archaeological guided tour. You may be somewhat familiar with it. This year, we had planned a trip to Athens for a week as the Greek Bronze Vase exhibit is conducive to such a destination." He raised his eyeglasses up to the window, inspecting the lenses he'd cleaned, and put them back on.

"Yes, I'm familiar with the summer guided tours," Curt said, straightening his back against the chair and placing his hands over his knees. "Robert's parents took one and absolutely loved it."

Dr. Jones smiled and shook his head. "Dr. Lisa Gould, one of the curators with the Antiquities department, will be leading the guided tour this year. But she needs help." He placed the cleaning cloth back inside the drawer. "Unfortunately, our volunteer who helps out with the tours won't be able to fly anytime soon. It's a last-minute request; that's why I'm asking if the two of you can go together. If only one of you can go, we'll work with that as well." He placed his elbows on the desk and clasped his hands.

"I'm absolutely ecstatic, Dr. Jones!" Curt said, rubbing his hands together. He looked at me and winked.

"You have been doing a terrific job during your internship this summer. And your teachers at the university have provided me with excellent recommendations for both of you. At this point, I can't think of anyone more qualified for this opportunity. We have only three weeks, and while I don't want to pressure you, I need an answer no later than the end of this week. I believe it will be an invaluable experience for both of you if you accept to volunteer as guides for this educational program." He adjusted his eyeglasses on his face and nodded.

"Thank you, Dr. Jones," I said. "It's so nice of you to think about us. My only concern is that I have to go back to teaching in exactly three weeks." How could I seize this opportunity to go to Greece and see Nikos without jeopardizing my job?

"It shouldn't be an issue, Sabrina. I'll talk with the art school's principal. We'll arrange a substitute teacher to replace you for a couple of weeks." Dr. Jones sounded as if he'd already thought of any detail which might hinder me from accepting his offer.

I shook my head. "If that's the case," I said, "I can tell you right now I'd love to. I can't thank you enough for this invitation. I've always wanted to go to Greece and visit the archaeological sites. I'm honored you thought about me, Dr. Jones. Thank you again."

Curt stood up from the chair and put his hands in his pockets. "I'm at a total loss for words right now, Dr. Jones. This is beyond my wildest dreams. There's no way I'd pass this up. Count me in for sure. Thank you."

"Then," Dr. Jones said, "I believe we're settled. Thank you for your willingness to take on this last-minute request. Roxanne will work on the flight and hotel reservations. She will email you about any other requirements and any paperwork you need to sign. We will also need copies of your passports—I assume both of you have valid passports, correct?"

We both nodded. Dr. Jones stood up and directed us to Roxanne. We spent the next few minutes talking to her about the trip's logistics. I couldn't wait to tell Nikos I'd be in Athens in three weeks.

Before going back to our departments, Curt gave me a tight hug.

"You're going to see him earlier than you thought, girlfriend. I'm so happy for you!"

"This is a dream, Curt. I still can't believe we're going to Greece. This is surreal." I hugged him back. We were like two children jumping up and down after opening Christmas presents.

"Robert and Jane are going to die. We should go for happy hour at Provisions after work. We need a drink to celebrate. What do you say?"

"It sounds great. I need a drink right now, but I guess I'll wait 'til five." I chuckled. "See you later at Provisions."

"Don't say anything to Robert and Jane. I'll tell them we're going for happy hour, and we'll deliver the news there," Curt said before leaving.

The rest of the day flew by. Soon it was five o'clock, and we gathered at the trendy restaurant's bar for happy hour. I was so excited, I decided to try something new and different. I ordered the Adonis, a delicious concoction of Palo Cortado sherry, sweet vermouth, and bitters with hints of vanilla. Curt and Robert ordered the tap beer special, and Jane settled for a glass of white wine. The bartender brought us an order of their freshly made hot breadsticks.

"Are we celebrating something?" Jane narrowed her eyes and threw her hands up in the air. "You two have kept me in the dark for too long after talking to Dr. Jones this afternoon."

"It's well worth the wait, my lovely. You won't believe what we have to tell you." Curt raised his beer glass for a toast. I touched his glass with mine, and Robert and Jane joined in.

"Sabrina and I are going to Greece."

Jane's wine glass almost dropped from her hand. Robert's eyes seemed to pop out of their sockets.

"What?" they asked in unison.

Curt showed them his beautiful dimples. He looked like an angel.

"We're going to be tour guides for the museum's tour of Athens with Dr. Lisa Gould. The docent who usually accompanies her is unable to go, and Dr. Jones invited us to tag along and help. What do you think? Isn't it simply fa-bu-lous?"

Three

AFTER I HAD DRUNK more than I probably should have at Provisions, my head spun slightly and a rush of happiness invaded my thoughts. In a few weeks, I'd be in Nikos's arms. It was too good to believe, and I wanted to tell Nikos about my impending trip. I got into the shower first to sober up a little bit so I wouldn't sound as if I were a blushing teenager when I called him. And it was better to call him when he was waking up, not when he was still dreaming.

Three long rings later, I heard his raspy, smoky voice. He sounded as if he'd just woken up. The shower didn't help me much, and the alcohol was still making me tipsy. As soon as I heard his voice, my legs shook like jelly and my heart skipped a beat.

"Hi, Nikos. It's me, Sabrina. Did I wake you up?" I asked, afraid I had disturbed him.

"Are you okay?" His tone made me melt. The moisture in between my legs made me dizzy with desire. I could barely articulate my words. I wished I hadn't drunk so much.

"I have something to tell you." My voice faltered. There was a second of silence before I heard him again.

"What happened?" He sounded worried.

"Dr. Jones invited me to go with the museum's tour to Greece," I blurted out. "I'll be in Athens in about three weeks."

"Congratulations, Sabrina. You deserve this more than anyone. You're a great student; this is truly exciting." His tone sounded robotic, somehow unemotional.

I bit my lower lip and lowered my head. I had expected a different reaction from him. I wanted him to be as excited as I was that we would see each other again soon. Instead, his answer reminded me I was a student, not his lover.

"Thank you. I . . . I'm so looking forward to it. I can't believe I will see you in a few weeks." A lump formed in my throat. The effects of the alcohol lingered, and my palms were sweaty.

"It will be a wonderful experience for you. I'm sure you will enjoy helping Dr. Gould. She's been here many times, and you can learn a lot from her."

I wanted him to say he was looking forward to spending all his time with me. *Get to your senses, Sabrina.* I knew he was busy and it would be hard to see him while he was working and dealing with his family and the theft of the jewels. But I ached for him, and my reasoning remained in the background, refusing to surface.

"I hope I can spend as much time as possible with you when I'm not with the group," I mumbled.

"I do, too, Sabrina. But keep in mind things here are hectic right now; I don't want to promise you anything I may not be able to honor. Being with you in Athens and showing you around would be unforgettable. I'd love to have time to be with you."

What am I thinking? I can't be disappointed with this man. He's what I've always wanted. I need to stop being so ridiculously insecure about whatever he says or does. He's telling me what I want to hear, isn't he? And he's being realistic about it as well. I can't complain; he's real, he's honest; he's the love of my life.

"When Dr. Jones offered me the opportunity to take this trip, I didn't even think twice. Being with you is all I want." I walked toward my bedroom window and closed the curtains. The shadows from the street lights disappeared, and I turned on the bedside lamp.

"I'm glad you accepted it, and I'm sure this will be invaluable for your studies. Sabrina." He paused after saying my name. I heard him sigh as if preparing to say something I didn't want to hear. I waited for him to continue. "I don't want you to jeopardize your experience. You were offered this opportunity because Dr. Jones believes in you. And your knowledge of Greek culture is exceptional. You need to focus to be able to give one hundred percent of yourself to this project. Your priority in Greece should not be to see me."

I sighed, trembling while I held the phone. What did he mean by that? Didn't he want to see me while I was in Greece? He was lecturing me as if I were a student.

"Nikos, I thought you'd be happy that I'm coming . . . I thought you'd want to be with me." I let myself fall on the bed and stared at the ceiling.

"I do, Sabrina. You have no idea how I feel about you right now. I wish you were here with me. I wish it were you instead of Maggie who had come to Greece with me. I wish I could whisk you away to Mikonos, Naxos, Crete, Corfu, any island, and forget about all of this. I want to be with you. But . . ." He paused again.

Was he measuring his words? I heard him sigh. I pictured him pacing around, his masculine fingers combing through his hair in agitation. He'd said what I wanted to hear from him. Yet there was a *but*. And I didn't want to hear the *but* part of it. He had me wrapped around his finger from the first day I saw him. I was his, unconditionally. His presence alone was enough to make me melt and surrender to him. Not being with him was something I couldn't fathom. *My love, my dream, what is keeping you from me? Why is there a but?*

"But what, Nikos? I'm yours. You have me. I don't want anyone else but you."

"I told you before I don't want to hurt you in any way, Sabrina. I've already done enough damage, and I'm not happy about it. Leaving under these circumstances was not how I wanted to part from you. And I don't want to part from you. But this is not easy. I'm worried about your feelings and the reality of our lives."

I curled up in bed like a scared child. I knew my faltering voice would reveal my shock.

"What are you trying to tell me? What damage? What reality? Maybe it's better if I don't go." I realized what a stupid thing I'd said as soon as it came out of my mouth. I shouldn't have called him after drinking. I hit my forehead with the palm of my hand.

"Why wouldn't you come? Don't do anything because of me, Sabrina. Don't destroy your goals and your opportunities because of me. Don't. You must take this trip. It will only help you in your career."

"Nikos, I can't go to Greece if I won't spend time with you." I rolled over.

"You will see me, Sabrina. Of course you will see me. But don't get things confused. I want you, but you're coming here to work. And I'm in hell dealing with the jewels right now. The situation was already bad with the museum, and as I told you before, I'm busy with my family too. Unfortunately, it seems to be an awful time for us to be together."

"I understand," I acquiesced. What else could I say? Was he being protective of me, of him, or of both of us? I didn't need his protection against my feelings. I thought I had prepared myself to suffer for him, and I'd go to the end of the world to be with him, no matter what it took. Unless he told me he didn't want me. At least that didn't seem to be the case.

"I have to go now, my beautiful. I'm taking Maggie to the airport. She's flying back today. Listen, if I were Hades, I'd kidnap you and take you away with me to my underworld, my Persephone. Away from it all."

He managed to make me smile.

"Kidnap me, then. Take me away to an island as you said. I'll be the happiest prisoner ever." I stared dreamily at the ceiling.

"Don't tease me. You're not here to satiate my desire for you. Sleep well. I'll talk to you soon."

He hung up. The silence didn't ease my confusion. What was happening? Inebriated, I felt like I was on an emotional rollercoaster again. What would I do? My excitement about the trip to Greece had come to a halt. It wasn't how I'd expected him to react when I told him about it. But I had to stop overanalyzing the situation. And I had to stop second-guessing Nikos's every word. He said he wanted me.

But he was too busy—or was that just an excuse? Puzzled, I drifted off to sleep. I was hoping to dream of Nikos as the mighty Hades kidnapping his beloved Persephone. Instead, thoughts of him taking Maggie to the airport permeated my restless slumber.

The next day, while we were having lunch, Curt mentioned Maggie was coming back to Houston. It was hard to believe he always found out about what happened in the museum before anyone else. I pretended I didn't know. I didn't want to tell them about the weird conversation I'd had with Nikos the night before while I was still half-drunk. Thankfully, Jane didn't ask me whether I'd talked to him yet. She assumed I had been too tipsy to bother calling him.

Although I wasn't in my best mood, I managed to conceal it from my friends. The emotional rollercoaster I was on with Nikos was driving me insane. And I knew exactly what Jane would say—that I had to stay away from him. In a way, she was right. He was back in his own environment. A week in Greece wouldn't do anything to improve our relationship. Even if—or when—he came back to Houston, it would be a temporary arrangement. His work and his life were in Athens, and mine were in Houston. But I didn't want to think about it. Not yet. I was not ready to give him up. There had to be a way. I was hoping we'd somehow be together or find a way to strengthen our relationship. I needed more time with him. Hell, I needed the rest of my life with him.

"So, Mr. Know-It-All, when is Maggie coming back?" Jane asked Curt.

"I heard she's flying back today, so we might guess she's going to be here tomorrow." He smirked.

"Oh, no, I'm not ready for her." Robert shook his head. "She will be boasting about Greece, Nikos, the stolen jewels, and her father's private plane. Zeus, help us!"

We all laughed.

"Look at the bright side, Robert." Jane nudged him with her elbow. "She'll tell us what we want to know about this crazy story. Actually, I can't wait to see her and hear what she will be babbling about!"

"Yes, I'm dying of curiosity. I want to know what is going on before we fly to Athens. I'm glad she won't be there when we go. Right, Sabrina?"

I barely heard Curt. I was distracted watching a delivery man walk into the restaurant carrying a beautiful bouquet of exquisite flowers in a glass vase. He stopped at a table where some of our internship colleagues were having lunch and showed them a card. They pointed him toward our table. We stared at each other as the delivery man approached us.

"Miss Sabrina?" he asked. All eyes landed on me.

I nodded. "Yes, I'm Sabrina."

"This is for you," he said, offering me the lovely bouquet. "Please sign here; I need to confirm you've received it." He handed me a piece of paper. Jane took the vase from my arms, and as soon as I signed my name, the man left.

"For the love of Chloris, goddess nymph of flowers." Robert touched a flower petal as if he were touching a precious diamond. "What is this?"

"It looks like the bouquet of Persephone." Curt lowered his head to smell the flowers. We all gazed at the bouquet as Jane handed it back to me with a frown.

"Bouquet of Persephone? Are you kidding me? What does it mean?"

"See, Persephone and the nymphs were gathering flowers when she was abducted by Hades, right? These are the flowers she was gathering: roses, crocuses, violets, irises, lilies, and larkspur blooms." Curt pointed at each flower as he named them. "A most exquisite and unusual bouquet of flowers. If you observe carefully, there are even two pomegranates decorating the floral arrangement. It could only be put together by a Greek mythology connoisseur." Their eyes fell on me again.

"Do you care to explain, Miss Greek-mythology-lover?" Jane tipped her head and pointed at the vase. The blood was rushing to my face. The bouquet could only have been sent by Nikos. I stared at the flowers in disbelief and picked up the card tucked in with the blooms.

"Leave her alone." Curt nudged Jane, surprising me. "She needs to enjoy her beautiful flowers and read the card by herself. We all know it can only be from Nikos. Let's get out of here."

"Thanks, Curt." I looked down at the flowers, feeling my cheeks still burning hot.

"Well, you're off the hook for now. But I want all the details about this later." Jane picked up her empty lunch tray from the table. "Wow. This is amazing. The most beautiful bouquet I've ever seen. The bouquet of Persephone!"

I opened the card as soon as they were out of sight, breathing a sigh of relief thanks to Curt's timely discretion. I didn't want to read the card and find out why Nikos was sending me a bouquet of Persephone in front of anyone.

I'll take all the time I can to be with you. I can't wait to make love to you again. You're my goddess, and I want you, my Persephone.

I closed my eyes, holding the card and inhaling the delicious fragrance of the dazzling flowers. How was it possible for me not to love this man? I looked at the velvety pink, purple, light lavender, blue, vivid indigo, and white hues of the colorful flowers, contrasting exquisitely with the two plump red pomegranates—so carefully chosen, so carefully put together. *Oh, Nikos, please don't give me up. When you're not around, my world is not the same.*

Jumping with joy, I went back to the gallery. My coworkers and the curator were amazed by the loveliness of my bouquet. They'd never seen such a striking arrangement before. I put the vase on the floor close to where I was setting up one of the displays. While I completed my task, I feasted my eyes on the wonderful flowers and took pleasure in knowing I'd soon be in his arms again. And in his bed.

It didn't take long for the afternoon to be over and for Jane to come running to my department before I headed out.

"Okay, Sabrina, enough of this mystery. It was hard to work the whole afternoon thinking about your bouquet of Persephone. What happened?"

I smiled at her, shaking my head. "You're impossible, Miss

Curiosity. I'll tell you about it when we get home." I picked up the vase and walked with Jane to the parking lot.

"You look ridiculously blissful. But who wouldn't?"

She followed me home in her car, and when we got to my place, she held the door for me to carry the vase inside. I placed it carefully in the center of the table in my living room. I was in another world, smelling the fragrance of the flowers the goddess Demeter had created for her daughter Persephone, who was gathering them before the mighty Hades fell in love with her and abducted her to his underworld. The musky, romantic, and strong smell of the roses, mixed with the subtle fruity and floral notes of the other blooms, made me feel like a goddess. Only Nikos could do this to me.

But something still made me uncomfortable about our relationship.

"So?" Jane pressed, bringing me back from my wild garden dream.

"They're from Nikos," I whispered, still in a love-induced stupor.

"Of course they are. That's obvious. But why did he send you this? For example, what is the meaning of the bouquet of Persephone? I can't believe Curt knew it. He certainly is an expert in mythology." She made herself comfortable on the couch.

"Yes, he is. I'm not sure I would have recognized it but for the pomegranates. You know, the only fruit Persephone ate while she was a prisoner of Hades in the underground."

"Yes, yes, I know this. Tell me what is going on." She leaned forward and touched the soft petal of one of the roses.

I rolled my eyes. "You're so impatient!"

"Have you talked to him? Did you tell him you're going to Greece in a few weeks?" She glided the tips of her fingers delicately over the different flowers, feeling their velvety touch.

"Yes. I told him."

"And?" She brought her face closer to the bouquet and smelled it, closing her eyes.

"I don't know. At first, his reaction wasn't what I'd expected. But then he kind of lit up and sent me the flowers, so it's all good."

"Okay, that's not a story. What do you mean his reaction was not what you expected? Just open up. Come on, Sabrina, what's going on between you two?" She leaned back on the couch and hugged her knees.

"Maybe you can help me figure it out. I was so excited when I called him last night to tell him about the trip, right? But he didn't exactly jump for joy when he heard the news. He told me I had to focus on the work I'd be doing there because my priority was not to be with him. It was disappointing. But I was tipsy. I think I overreacted." I leaned forward, putting my elbows on my knees, and rested my face on my hands.

"You should've known better. I told you he was playing with you while he was here. Now he's back in his environment and you're not a toy in his reach anymore. He has his life."

"I'm in love with him, Jane. I can't deny it. I told him how disappointed I was when he didn't seem excited about seeing me. Then he said he wished he could kidnap me to one of the Greek islands to get away from our problems. That's why Persephone and Hades's story came up." I got up and started pacing around the living room.

"That's why he sent you the flowers, then? I get it. The dark lord of the underworld wants to break your heart and kill you. Did you have an argument over the phone?"

"No, we didn't argue. It was just a weird vibe, I guess. He realized he made me upset and tried to make me feel better. Read the card." I took the card that came with the flowers from my purse and gave it to Jane.

"Oh, the ever-elusive, charming, seductive Greek god. So why can't he run away with you? Should I guess? Work, long distance, Maggie . . ." She waved the card around.

"No, he's not with Maggie. He was taking her to the airport after we spoke. She might be in town by now." I took the card back from her and placed it on the table next to the vase.

"Wait, wait, wait . . . Rewind a little bit. So you told him you were going to Greece and he wasn't excited about it. Then, he regretted what he said when you got upset by his lack of enthusiasm. All this while Maggie was still there? Maybe even by his side? And when she leaves, he sends you this enticing message with the most alluring flowers a lover could ever send? It doesn't sound good." She shook her head.

"What do you mean?" I sat back on the loveseat facing her.

"You're blinded by love; you can't see it. I hate to wake you up, because you're so in love with this guy it hurts." She clenched her fists and hit her thighs with them. "But he's nothing but a manipulative, tempting, phony womanizer."

"Why are you saying this? He's not." It sickened me to hear her saying this about him. I couldn't see Nikos the same way she did. He had been mine, and to think he was touching other women the same way was horrifying to even contemplate. It was hard for me to understand why Jane held Nikos in such low esteem. She stood up from the sofa and paced around the room, staring at me wide-eyed before throwing her arms up.

"He is playing you, Sabrina. Can't you see?" She raised her voice. "As soon as Maggie left Greece, he sent you flowers. He's free now! He didn't want to commit to being with you in Greece until he was sure she was flying back to Houston. It's so clear to me now. But you won't believe me, will you?"

I picked up the card from the table and read it again. My palms were sweating, and my heart was pounding hard. Tears filled my eyes. Was it possible?

"It's not him. He wouldn't have written this if he didn't mean it . . ."

"Don't fool yourself. Nikos is bad news. I've been saying this for a while now." She stood in front of me. "And the more I read into it, the more I realize I'm right. You asked me to help you figure it out; well, now you have it."

"I can't accept your theory, Jane. I know what you're going to say. Maybe you're right. Maybe he's playing with me. But I don't see him like this. I have to believe him. Believe he's telling me the truth and he wants me next to him as much as I do." A tear escaped and rolled down my face while the choking thickness in my throat muffled my words. Jane stood still in front of me.

"I'm so sorry, my sweet, dreamy friend. I shouldn't have been so inconsiderate. I sometimes fail to realize how much you're in love with this guy. He's a god indeed. He has these alluring, piercing eyes and smoldering looks and everything about him—oh, yes. The guy is to die for, and I understand it's hard not to fall for him. Oh, Sabrina. I don't know what to do to help you."

She crouched on the floor and gave me a hug.

"Thank you, Jane. You're my best friend, and you only want to help. My instincts tell me to run, but my heart's pulling me toward him and I have no strength to push back. I need some time by myself to think this through." My voice returned to normal as I regained my composure. She let me go, and a tender smile sprouted on her beautiful, concerned face.

"I hope you feel better. And as always, if you want to talk—if you need me—you know where to reach me. Call me anytime."

She picked up her purse and left, leaving me alone with my beautiful bouquet of Persephone and my tumultuous thoughts. I wanted to be with Nikos. I wanted to believe what he was telling me. I read the card again and stared at the gorgeous flowers. I turned on Pandora to break the eerie silence. Carolina Liar's "Show Me What I'm Looking For" came on, matching the words with my feelings. Yes, I needed to be saved from my confusion. *Yes, Nikos, please show me what I'm looking for.* Was this a sign? I wanted to believe it. I wanted to believe the song. It played on just as I needed to hear some magical advice on how to interpret my relationship with and my feelings for Nikos.

I wiped away the thin stream of tears rolling down my face and kneeled on the floor in front of the flowers. I touched their petals, allowing their velvety softness to caress the tips of my fingers. I loved the warmth, the sweetness, the fragrance, and the uniqueness of each flower. Only a passionate, intense man would be able to come up with such a romantic idea. I refused Jane's theory. I wanted him more than ever. He was mine. But did he want me as much as I wanted him?

Four

I HAD A GOOD night's sleep despite the convoluted feelings Nikos's flowers brought upon me. Having them by my bedside helped me tune out any weird thoughts. After a dreamless night, I woke up refreshed and ready to take on the day. Curt and I were having a meeting with both Dr. Jones and Dr. Gould to square away some of the details of our trip. I didn't call Nikos or send him a thank you note for the flowers. *I'll keep him wondering what I think about them.*

Roxanne asked us to have a seat and wait, as Dr. Jones had to fit an unexpected guest into his schedule at the last minute. He'd see us as soon as he was finished. About five minutes later, the door to his office opened. Maggie came out, dressed in a turquoise-blue midriff top and skinny white jeans. She looked stunning as usual, and I was as insecure as ever, realizing she'd been with Nikos the day before.

"Maggie, what a pleasure to see you, darling!" Curt jumped off the sofa to hug her. She hugged him back and turned her glassy, Medusa eyes on me with all her hatred.

"How was the trip to Greece, beautiful?" Curt asked, releasing her.

"Stressful, to say the least." Her stare was locked on me. "The jewels haven't been found yet. But my marvelous Nikos is working

27

nonstop to get to the bottom of this horror. He's a dream. What would I do without him?"

I bit my lower lip and looked away from her, staring out the window. I didn't want to hear this woman talk about *my* Nikos as if he were *hers*.

"Any clues?" Curt glanced furtively at me when he perceived the way Maggie had provoked me.

"Not yet. Interpol is on the case, so it should only be a matter of days before we get something. It has messed up Nikos's schedule here. But Dad will assist him and the museum as needed. What are you doing here? Are you talking to Dr. Jones?" she asked, realizing we were waiting our turn.

"Yeah. Mind you, Dr. Jones has asked us to go to Greece in a few weeks to help Dr. Gould with the guided tour of Athens. My dream trip." He rubbed his hands excitedly.

"Both of you? Why does Dr. Gould need both of you to babysit her tourists?" Her eyes searched mine with the striking intensity of a barbaric cyclops.

"Well, see, the volunteer can't make it. Dr. Jones thought it was a better idea to send both of us since it's our first time. I can't wait to see Athens!"

I bit my lower lip again, attempting to control a growing urge to slap Maggie in the face. I despised her arrogance.

Roxanne saved me from the cruel Medusa. "Dr. Jones is ready for you two. Could you please step into his office?" I got up from the chair and followed Curt. I was walking past Maggie when she grabbed my arm.

"Don't you think for a second you're going to Athens to enjoy a honeymoon with Nikos. I've warned you before; leave him alone. I'm not entertaining the idea of you going there with the excuse of being a guide for the museum. Stay away from my man!"

I yanked my arm from her grip. "Leave me alone. You have no right to threaten me or to dictate who I can see. Excuse me. Dr. Jones is waiting for me."

Butterflies danced in my stomach. I hated confronting Maggie, and I couldn't stand it when she talked about Nikos in such a possessive, jealous way, intimidating me. Without looking back, I entered Dr. Jones's office and took a seat next to Curt.

Dr. Jones raised his eyebrows. "Can I get you some water, Sabrina? You look a little flustered. Are you feeling well?"

"I'm fine, Dr. Jones. Thanks." I took a deep breath to regain my composure. "I'm . . . I'm just excited about the trip." I leaned back in the chair, trying to relax.

Curt glanced at me, reached for my hand, and squeezed it hard. "We're both eager, Dr. Jones. We can't wait."

"Good. I'm glad you're all on board. I'm sorry to keep you waiting. Maggie returned from Greece yesterday. She came to give me a personal report of what is transpiring over there."

"Is Dr. Soulis coming back?" Curt asked.

"We'd love for him to come back. But it doesn't seem he'll be able to travel anytime soon. According to Maggie, the situation is rather complicated. We'll do what we can to help him out. Anyhow, Dr. Gould is joining us in a few minutes. In the meantime, I want to go over the itinerary with you."

After telling Roxanne we shouldn't be interrupted for the next hour, he closed the door. And he didn't mention anything else about Nikos.

When we left the meeting, Curt invited me for coffee in the break room.

"Sabrina, you were white as a ghost when you entered Dr. Jones's office. What did Medusa say to you?" he asked once we'd sat down with our cups of coffee.

"You're such a sweetie, Curt. I appreciate your concern. You know Maggie . . . she's used to getting her way. And it seems I'm in her way." I sipped my coffee.

"Yes, it's Nikos, I know. You don't have to tell me what's going on with you and him. I mean, after the flowers he sent you yesterday, I so get it, my love. Such a bouquet! What man would do something like this? He's a Greek god, for sure." He tapped my hands lightly with his fingers.

"Thank you for leaving when I got the flowers. I needed the time. But it's complicated, Curt. Nikos lives in Greece. And Maggie . . ." I paused, stirring the coffee with a spoon.

"Did she threaten you again?" He took a sip of his coffee.

"She told me to stay away from him. Do you think they're indeed dating?" My voice faltered at the question.

"Baby, you're stressing out. Don't be afraid of Maggie. Go for our Hades. He's a dream. And I think he likes *you*, not her. I wish Robert would have the sensibility to send me a bouquet of Persephone." Curt illuminated the whole room with an enthusiastic laugh. His beautiful blond, curly hair accentuated his angelic features. "I'll get more information from Maggie about our god. And"—he got closer to me and lowered his voice—"I'll cover for you in Athens if needed, so you can see the mighty one."

I gave a loud laugh and slapped him lightly on the arm.

"Don't be naughty, Curt!"

He winked and blew me a kiss.

"That's what friends are for, my lovely. And I can't get over that bouquet. It's so awesome. Lucky you."

We left the break room laughing and returned to our areas to finish the work for the day. The quick coffee break with Curt had energized me. I dismissed any bad vibes I had about Maggie and Nikos and my own weird insecurities.

When I got home, the gorgeous flowers reminded me I hadn't thanked Nikos yet. I had to wait a few hours to call him. The time difference was so annoying. I turned on the TV to look for something interesting to watch. A special program about Greece was on the Travel Channel. Just what I needed. It was futile to try to escape Nikos's world. The beautiful Cape Sounion was on the screen, highlighting the magnificent and romantic sunset over the Aegean Sea.

Cape Sounion was about forty-three miles from Athens. It was one of the most sought-after day trip excursions from the capital. According to the legend, Theseus promised his father, King Aegeus, he'd hoist a white sail upon his return from Crete if he killed the Minotaur. Although he defeated the beast, Theseus forgot about his promise. When King Aegeus saw the black sail on the horizon, he assumed his son was dead and leaped to his death. Tragic, like most Greek stories. Nonetheless, it was one of the most emotional places in Greece for lovers of mythology. Thinking about how I'd love to go there with Nikos and see the spectacular sunset with him, I dozed off. When I woke up, curled on my couch with the TV still on, it was about three in the morning. Perfect time to call Nikos. It was not what I'd had in mind, but at least he'd be awake. It rang twice before he answered.

"Hello, Sabrina. What are you doing awake at three in the morning?" His tone was serious and concerned.

"Hi, Nikos . . . I fell asleep while watching a special about Greece on the Travel Channel." I chuckled. "I wanted to call you to thank you for the bouquet of Persephone. I love it. It's the most beautiful flower arrangement I've ever seen."

"I'm glad you liked it," I heard his husky voice say. "How are you?"

"Much better now that I'm talking with you. Has your brother come home yet?"

I heard him sigh before answering. "My mother received a text from him telling her he's fine. Nothing else. She's beside herself with worry. I need to find out where the text was sent from. The detectives working on the case of the jewels offered to help me."

"Are you at work?" I stretched my legs out on the couch.

"Yes, I'm at the museum right now. Interpol is here investigating, so some sections of the museum are off-limits to the public. And the financial situation is another matter I have to deal with. The only good news I have is from my archaeological team. They've been doing excavations in Amphipolis, a town in the northern part of the country, and found a large tomb. We suspect it dates back to Alexander the Great's reign. If it is, it's of major historical significance."

"Wow! I'd love to see it. Is it from around the late fourth century BC?"

"Yes. I'll have to go there at some point. I'm the chief archaeologist and team director. I'm expected to lead the research, do a press conference, things like that. But I'm not sure when yet. At least this finding may yield some resources and financing to our research. Speaking of research, how are you coming along with yours?"

I shifted on the couch. "Well, not a lot of progress since you left. But I'll work on it to keep myself busy before coming to Greece. I saw Maggie yesterday, and she . . ." I hesitated. I shouldn't have mentioned her. It would only upset him.

"And she what?" I sensed the haste in his answer.

"The usual. She told me to stay away from her man. You."

A grunt interrupted an uncomfortable second of silence before he spoke again. "I'm not her man. I've told you this before. She thinks she owns me. She has the money we need to survive the crisis in the museum, but I'm not hers. I have business with her and her father, that's all."

I bit my lips. "I can't help feeling insecure when she says it, though. She was there with you and—"

"Sabrina," he interrupted me with a serious tone. "Did you read the card I sent you with the flowers?"

"Yes, of course, I did. Why?" I switched the phone to my other ear.

"Do you believe my words?"

I picked up the card sitting on the table and read it again before answering him.

"I want to. I need to believe your words."

"Then do. That's how I feel about you. I wouldn't lie about it. Don't let Maggie or anyone else fill your mind with rumors or whatever. I'll show you how I feel about you when you're here."

I closed my eyes to savor the warmth of his words.

"I'd love to go to Cape Sounion with you. Would you take me there?" I asked on a whim.

"Sure. Whatever you want, my beautiful."

"I want you, Nikos. I can't wait to breathe your fragrance again and taste your mouth. I wish my trip was today." I stretched out on the couch, looking dreamily at the ceiling.

"You'll be in my arms soon enough. Now go get some sleep

before you head to the museum this morning. Fill me in on the details of your flight, hotel, and itinerary as soon as it's all finalized. I'll work around my schedule to see you. Don't worry if you don't hear much from me in the meantime. It's chaotic around here now, and I may have to go to Amphipolis for a few days to inspect the site."

"Please be careful, and good luck with your projects. I miss you." The line went dead. Nikos was gone, leaving within me a vacuum only he could fill. I read his card again.

I'll take all the time I can to be with you. I can't wait to make love to you again. You're my goddess, and I want you, my Persephone.

Five

THE DAYS BEFORE THE trip moved more slowly than I wanted, but at least I had enough activities to keep me busy. Dr. Jones and Dr. Gould finalized our itinerary. We were staying at the Athens Gate Hotel, located in the historic district of the city. It sat opposite the Temple of Zeus and Hadrian's Gate, overlooking the Acropolis. A magnificent location, close to most of the sites we would be visiting.

Curt and I wanted rooms facing the Acropolis, but those were hard to reserve and had a waitlist spanning several months. I texted the itinerary information to Nikos. Besides that, I hadn't heard much from him since our last phone conversation.

The Arts of Africa, Oceania, and the Americas curatorial department finally reopened the gallery with a great party, coinciding with the celebration of our successful internship. It had, without a doubt, been one of the best professional and educational experiences of my life—with the added bonus of having met Nikos.

The Greek Vases exhibit would be showing until the end of the year. Dr. Jones was confident Nikos would come back before December to organize its transfer to the Atlanta Museum of Art, where it was going next.

It was finally time to say goodbye to the summer and restart our normal lives. Two days before we would fly to Greece, Curt and

Robert threw a "Goodbye, Summer" party at their place. I was more excited to attend this time around. After all, my last experience in their house hadn't been fun when Nikos and Maggie showed up as special guests. Curt couldn't stop talking about our imminent trip, and Jane had given up on asking me questions about Nikos nonstop. She knew by now there was nothing she could say to prevent me from seeing him.

And at last, Friday afternoon arrived, and we headed to the Intercontinental Airport to meet the group and fly to Greece. Robert and Curt drove to my apartment to pick me up, as Curt had insisted we go to the airport together. Jane tagged along. It amused me to see how Robert and Jane acted as if our one-week trip would last months. Dr. Gould met us at Terminal E with the museum members who had signed up for the trip.

After saying our goodbyes, we boarded KLM's Boeing 747 flight 662 for the nine-hour trip to Amsterdam. There, we'd have a four-hour layover before boarding KLM flight 1575 for another three-hour flight to Athens, scheduled to arrive around 4 p.m. local time on Saturday.

I took a sleeping pill in hopes of falling asleep fast. I didn't want the noises and lights of the flight to disturb me throughout the night. I needed to relax. The expectation of being in Nikos's arms in a few hours was overpowering. I was sure I'd be exhausted from the excitement, the long overnight flight, and jet lag.

Even though it was disappointing, I knew Nikos wasn't going to be at the airport waiting for me. I was with Dr. Gould and the group, and it would be awkward for him to show up at our arrival. Our transfer from the airport to the Athens Gate Hotel had been arranged in advance by the museum. I hoped to hook up with Nikos later after settling at the hotel. The official program of our tour wouldn't begin until Monday, and I was glad we'd have the rest of Saturday and all of Sunday free to roam the city as we pleased.

As we stepped out of the airport terminal into the passenger pick up area to wait for our transportation to the hotel, I was assaulted by smog and fumes from the hectic Athens traffic. A hot, humid breeze carried along the sounds of car horns, police whistles, sirens, blasting radios, and tumultuous voices speaking in a language I didn't understand. Small cars sitting in convoluted traffic and harried pedestrians smoking and talking on their cells completed this assault on my senses. It was not what I had expected Athens to be like. It was overwhelming in an exotic way. I inhaled and took in the myriad of colors, sounds, and smells as a welcome change that would only enrich my life. And I hoped to have my god waiting for me at the other side of this archaeologically modern rainbow.

After the twelve-mile ride from the airport to the hotel, we were shown to our rooms to settle in for the evening. Curt was unable to sleep during the flight and all he wanted was to take a hot shower and curl up in bed. His room was directly across from mine, which was a bit odd. The other guests' rooms were all on the same side, facing the back street of the hotel. I gave Curt a peck on the cheek and headed to my room.

When I opened the door, I found a simple room with modern decor. Black-and-white pictures of Greek landmarks hung on the light beige walls. The furniture consisted of a comfortable-looking queen-size black-frame bed and a small, black round table with two lavender-colored chairs. On top of the table, a silver vase was filled with beautiful white tulips. A tray of fresh fruits had been carefully placed on one of the bedside tables.

I walked toward the balcony and pulled the curtains aside and found myself face to face with a magnificent view of the Acropolis. I stared at it wide-eyed. I couldn't believe I'd been this lucky. We were told the rooms facing the Acropolis had to be reserved months ahead of time. There had been no availability. I marveled at the spectacular view I'd somehow been blessed with.

"Room service!" A heavily accented voice called from the other side of the door after two knocks. *They must have gotten the wrong room.* I opened the door to find a hotel employee standing there with a rolling cart. Before I could protest, he entered the room, put a silver-plated bucket filled with ice on the table, set a bottle of champagne inside the bucket, and placed two flutes next to it.

"I'm sorry," I said. "I didn't order anything. You must have the wrong room."

The friendly-looking young man took a paper from his uniform pocket and looked at it. "Aren't you Miss Sabrina?"

I nodded, raising my eyebrows.

"Then I have the right room. Welcome to Athens and enjoy your stay."

I didn't want to argue with him about it. It would be better to find out who the rightful recipient of the champagne was later, so I picked up my purse in search of a few Euros to tip him with.

"Don't bother, Miss Sabrina. It's been taken care of." He waved his hands. "Courtesy of Dr. Soulis. Have a good evening. Kalispera."

My mouth dropped open. He smiled back at me, bowed his head, and excused himself, closing the door as he left. Nikos! I approached the table and looked at the expensive bottle in front of me. A small envelope I hadn't noticed sat next to the bucket, my name on the outside.

Enjoy the view, my goddess. I'll come by at 7 to take you to dinner on your first night in Athens. Welcome to my world.

I kissed the card and spun around, letting myself fall onto the comfortable bed, smiling like a happy child in front of a candy store. I had no reason not to trust Nikos.

I peeked at the clock and realized it was already six in the evening, local time. I had to get ready right away! I unpacked as fast as I could, hanging my clothes and tucking away my shoes and personal hygiene items. After a refreshing and energizing shower, I dried my hair, put on some light makeup, and chose a plain black dress with spaghetti straps. As a final touch, I dabbed Chance on my cleavage, behind my ears, and on my wrists. I was just about finished when there was a knock on the door.

"Welcome to Greece." Nikos was there, in front of me, impeccably dressed in a light-blue button-down shirt and light-gray trousers. His sleeves were slightly rolled up, showing a hint of his tanned and strong, muscled arms. He looked at me with those piercing eyes, emanating sexuality and desire. Before I could say anything, his big and strong hands cupped my face. His lips touched mine, arousing in me more desire than I could have hoped for.

His lusty lips nibbled on mine while his tongue tasted my half-opened mouth. I was breathless. I embraced his neck, drowning in his delicious signature fragrance. How I had missed his D&G Light Blue spicy, fresh, and sensual scent! With a hungry yearning, his tongue dove inside my mouth, teasing me while his hands roamed down my body, and he pulled me closer, embracing me with tenderness.

"Can you tell how much I want you?"

I couldn't hide my happiness.

"I can't believe I'm here with you. I think I'm dreaming."

He kissed my forehead and slid his hands down the back of my spine, sending a wave of hot desire to my groin. I was so ready for him. I was always ready for him.

"Nikos," I whispered, tightening my embrace. His mouth sought mine again, and he kissed me once more with an uncontrollable urge and then slowly let go. Holding my hand, he led me out onto the balcony.

The Acropolis looked like a vision from Olympus. I couldn't believe this was happening. Nikos stood behind me and brought me closer to him. He enveloped my waist with his arms and lowered his face to my bare neck. The touch of his lips on my skin sent shivers of pleasure down my spine, and a moan escaped my lips. The postcard-worthy perfection of the Acropolis framed this unforgettable sensation.

"Did you miss me?" he teased while his lips brushed against the nape of my neck and continued on to nibble on my earlobes.

"No," I whispered. "I didn't just miss you; I was dead without you and now I feel alive again and ready to love you."

"I will take this Chance." He lowered his head toward the side of my neck and inhaled the perfume I'd dabbed behind my ears. We stood still for a few minutes, admiring the staggering view in front of us. I wanted nothing else in the world but to be with this man. His hands glided from my waist to my breasts, and he cupped them with care, bringing me even closer to him. As he caressed me and kissed the nape of my neck, I moaned in delight, my nipples grew swollen, and I moved my hips closer to his. He turned me around and kissed me with desire. His tongue explored my mouth with an intense urgency, leaving me breathless, while his strong arms embraced me in a tight grip. My fingers tangled in his soft, wavy black hair. I was so dizzy with desire for him I almost fell when he released me.

"We should go." He took my hand and led me from the breezy balcony back into the room. Why would he do this when we were in the middle of a fiery kiss? I stopped before we reached the door, and he turned around to face me. As if guessing my protests, he placed his index finger against my lips.

"Don't say anything yet, my beautiful goddess. I want to take you to dinner first." His finger slid to the side of my cheek, and I closed my eyes, my skin tingling at his touch. His tongue brushed my lips before he bit the lower one, sending fires of desire down my spine. Gods of Olympus, how could I ever resist this man? I was beside myself. I yearned for him so much I could just explode. Now I had to wait until after dinner to have him. I picked up my purse and allowed him to lead the way to the elevator.

The concierge came toward us and offered Nikos his car keys as soon as we came out of the elevator.

"Dr. Soulis, the car is waiting outside. I hope we've met your expectations so far." He looked at me with respect and bowed. "Kalispera, Miss Sabrina. Enjoy the evening."

A metallic, dark-gray Jeep Compass waited for us in front of the hotel. Nikos opened the door for me and then took the driver's seat.

"The hotel staff seem to know you well," I said.

"Yes, they do. Whenever we have guests at the museum, or events in town, we use this hotel. The location is the best, and the service is excellent. They never refuse me a room with a view." He smirked and reached for my hand, bringing it up to his lips and kissing it.

"Is this where Maggie stayed? In a room with a view?"

He looked at me and frowned but didn't respond. How childish of me. Why did I have to bring Maggie into the conversation? On my first night with Nikos in Greece? After he got me a room with a view? I bit my lip so hard I almost broke the skin.

"Where are we going?" I changed subjects to ease the tension I'd created.

"The restaurant's name is Eleas Gi. It's one of the best Greek restaurants in Athens, and it has a fantastic view of the city. I made reservations for 7:30. I hope you're hungry."

"I'm hungry for you," I whispered, unable to disguise my craving for him any longer.

"I know." He looked at me with intensity. "But we can't be late. Someone is waiting for us."

"Someone's waiting for us?" Nikos was so unpredictable. Why didn't he tell me that at the hotel?

He caressed my hand. "I didn't want you to worry. I wanted to make sure you were comfortable when I came to the hotel."

"Who is it?" My voice shook.

"My mother."

My jaw dropped. "Your mother?"

"Don't feel nervous about meeting her. She's not feeling well lately. The Interpol agents helped me trace my brother's phone to a location in Cyprus. Mother is on the verge of a nervous breakdown. We have no idea what he's doing there or with whom. I'm doing what I can to entertain her and to be around her under the circumstances. I didn't want you to refuse to come to dinner with me because you knew my mother was coming along."

"I'd never refuse to meet your mother. It will be a pleasure. I'm sorry she's going through this. You should've told me. I'd love to have brought her flowers or something . . ."

His lips found my hand again. "Thank you for understanding."

After about a half-hour drive, we got to the place—an authentic Greek restaurant in Kifissia, a suburb of Athens. A restaurant employee opened the car door for me. After I stepped out, Nikos gave him the car keys before leading me through a corridor decorated with wine bottles. It seemed we were walking through paths of wine. At the end of the corridor, we were greeted by a smiling waiter who offered us a glass of tsipouro. What a magnificent and romantic atmosphere! I sipped the delicious anise-flavored Greek brandy and smiled at Nikos. I was glad I was able to have a sip of alcohol to relax before meeting his mother. I had no idea what Nikos had told her about me, and it was nerve-wracking to think about it.

The waiter led us toward the main room of the restaurant, where two impressive olive trees welcomed us. We passed through the classy dining room into a cozy open-air veranda. An enchanting view of Athens opened up as the main attraction. It was breathtaking. The place was simply magical.

Ms. Soulis waited for us at one of the tables on the veranda. She stood up as soon as she saw us, and I immediately noticed how Nikos resembled her. She was wearing a beautiful long-sleeve light-green dress and black dressy pumps. Ms. Soulis had Nikos's same dark, mysterious, and penetrating eyes framed by beautiful and natural long lashes. Her perfectly coiffed hair was arranged in a bun like a ballerina's. She was petite, slim, and gracious. It was easy to imagine her dancing and performing pirouettes in her youth. She had definitely taken care of her figure.

"Mother." Nikos embraced her and kissed her on the forehead. "Thanks for waiting. This is Sabrina, the American student I met at the museum in Houston." He opened his arm to allow me in closer.

I was shaking. The student was there again. *Okay, how else could he introduce me to his mother? Mother, this is my American lover?* I had to stop my ridiculous thoughts. I bowed to her respectfully. The beautiful, elegantly dressed woman gave me a warm smile and immediately put me at ease when she extended her hand to me.

"Kalispera, Sabrina," she greeted me with a heavy yet charming accent. "I'm so pleased to meet the girl who is melting away the icy walls surrounding the heart of my Nikos."

I raised my eyebrows.

"Mother!" Nikos snapped, trying to contain his reproachful tone. "Please."

"Oh, Nikos, she's so beautiful. With what's been happening now, it's a relief to meet such a lovely person," she said, ignoring his protests. "I'm sorry to impose my presence on your first night in Greece, Sabrina. Nikos is doing what he can to make me feel better, and I appreciate his efforts. I've been depressed lately."

"It's my pleasure, Ms. Soulis. I'm elated to meet you, and I'm sorry for what you're going through."

She took my hand warmly into hers. "You can call me Eleni if you prefer." She released me and motioned for us to sit down. While the waiter handed us menus, I finished my glass of tsipouro.

"Did you have a pleasant trip?" Ms. Soulis asked me.

"Yes, thanks for asking. I was actually able to sleep during the flight, but the jet lag will be upon me for the rest of the week." I opened the menu and flipped through the pages.

"By the time you're accustomed to the time zone, it will be time for you to leave," Nikos said. He had sported a worried frown from the moment his mother said I was the girl who was melting his heart. Did he regret the idea of bringing me to dinner with her? I hoped his distant demeanor wouldn't kill the sexual chemistry that had resurfaced when we saw each other again. I studied the menu, undecided about what to order. Nikos's air of preoccupation bothered me.

"May I suggest a dish for you, my dear?" his mother asked.

"Please do." I closed the menu. "The dishes sound delicious, and I have no idea what to order."

She proceeded to explain some of the mouth-watering Greek cuisine on the menu, all cooked with olive oil, the authentic taste of Greek cuisine. After we decided on what to eat, Nikos called over the waiter and ordered. The table was soon filled with an array of tasty appetizers—fluffy pita bread with olive oil and oregano, olive salad, smoked eggplant salad, mushroom pie baked in a wood oven with fresh aromatic herbs, and mushroom soup. While we munched on the appetizers and waited for the main course, Ms. Soulis asked me about my job, my degree, my upcoming graduation, and my plans for the future. Plans for the future? I peeked at Nikos, who was paying attention to the conversation in silence. What I wanted to tell her was that my plan for the future was to be with her son, no matter where, when, or how.

"I'd love to get a job in a museum and become a curator or maybe a museum director," I said instead.

She smiled at me. "Would you consider leaving your country and working overseas?"

I didn't want to look at Nikos. This sounded like a tricky question, and I wanted to give a suitable answer. Why did I feel she was interviewing me?

"If the right opportunity comes up and it's a good match, I'm sure I'd consider it." I avoided Nikos's stare. I could feel his hot gaze on me.

"It's good to know." Ms. Soulis took a sip of water. "I'd love for you to work with Nikos." She turned to her son. "I'm worried about your association with the lady who comes around here every once in a while. I wish you didn't have to work with her, Nikos."

"Mother, Maggie is a business associate. My relationship with her is purely professional. I can't dismiss her father's sponsorship of the museum right now." He crossed his arms and leaned back in his chair.

"I'm sorry, dear. You need to do what's best for you and for the museum." She gave him a light peck on the cheek and turned her attention back to me. "Would you work in Greece, Sabrina?"

"It'd be a dream if I could." I fidgeted with the napkin I'd placed on my lap. "This is my first time in Greece, and I've always wanted to visit. A week is not enough, but I hope I'll come back again."

"I'm sure you will." She patted my arm gently. "And my door is open for you at any time. You'll always be welcome here."

I nodded timidly. "Thank you. That's so lovely of you." I glanced at Nikos. The way he stared at me still hadn't changed. He had a worrisome expression, and his brows joined in a frown. What was he thinking?

The waiter brought our main dishes. The food was delicious, and I was glad Ms. Soulis had given me a wonderful suggestion. The conversation shifted to her. I listened in admiration as she told me the story of her life as a ballerina for the Greek National Opera Ballet and the aftermath of her husband's abandonment. She was indeed a strong-willed woman, but I saw signs of exhaustion of the warrior in her. The unexpected leaving of her younger son hadn't been easy on her at all. Although she was making an effort to enjoy the evening and put Nikos at ease, she was visibly shaken. Her eyes filled with tears whenever she talked about her younger son, and every single time Nikos reached for her hand and kissed her with affection, comforting her. Their relationship was of mutual respect, love, and admiration. It was easy to see why Nikos was so devoted to this woman and worried about her so much. Not only did he consider himself responsible for his mother, but he truly loved her, and she him.

"This food is simply delicious," I said. "Thank you for your suggestion. This magical place, the wonderful company, the food . . . I feel I'm a goddess of Olympus enjoying ambrosia."

Ms. Soulis laughed heartily. "I'm glad you're enjoying it," she said. "You've been a welcome distraction for me. I'm the one who needs to thank you for coming."

Nikos called over the waiter to take care of the check. In the meantime, his mother asked me to accompany her to the ladies' room. We excused ourselves and left the table.

"Sabrina, I want to thank you for coming tonight. Your presence has been a blessing to me. Can I ask you a favor?" she asked when we were by ourselves.

"It would be my pleasure to help you." I looked at her with curiosity.

"I don't know how to ask you this, but please be patient with my Nikos."

I raised my eyebrows and tilted my head, not quite comprehending what she meant.

"I'm sorry, but I don't think I understand your request, Ms. Soulis."

"Nikos lives for his work, Sabrina. He doesn't allow time for anything else in his life, and he's built a wall around his heart when it comes to love. He never got over the fact that his father left me for another woman. He swore he wouldn't commit to a relationship because he thinks love is suffering. There have been girlfriends of course, but it's never serious. Once, though, despite his fear of getting attached . . ." She lowered her head and looked down. "He fell in love."

What was she telling me? Who had Nikos fallen in love with? Was it Maggie? I stared at her, shaking inside, waiting for her to continue.

"He doesn't talk about it. It happened years ago, but it's left him with deep scars. He's tried to get over it by burying himself even more in his work. He keeps himself busy and avoids attachment and commitment at all cost." She rubbed her hands together.

I listened to her without blinking. Something hurtful had happened to Nikos, and he hadn't told me.

"The reason I'm telling you this is because I believe he's having a hard time dealing with his relationship with you."

"What happened to him?" Her words worried me.

"He needs to tell you, my dear. I can't. Unfortunately, it's up to him, and it's going to be tough for him to open his heart."

I nodded, understanding she was already revealing more than she should about Nikos's life. I wanted to know what had happened to him more than anything, but I knew she wouldn't betray him. As I remained silent, she continued.

"I thought he had finally broken the cycle of loneliness with Maggie. She comes here often, and they're always together—"

"He and Maggie are . . . together?" I interrupted her, my voice failing me. Why was she telling me this? Is this what she'd been trying to tell me all along? It was too much to take in one brief conversation.

"I'm not aware of the depth of their relationship. He doesn't tell me much about it except it is business-related. But . . ." She paused, took both my hands tightly in hers, and looked at me with sincerity. "It's not Maggie. It's you, Sabrina."

"Me?" I was appalled. What did she mean? Me what?

"Yes. You, Sabrina. It's you who's tearing him apart. I realized this as soon as he came back to Athens. I know my son." Her words paralyzed me.

"I'm . . . tearing him apart? How? I don't understand, I'm . . . oh, Ms. Soulis, I'm . . . I'm in love with Nikos." My confession came out as a whisper.

"Yes, my dear. I can tell. You just barely met, but there's something between the two of you which is undeniable. He's in love with you, too, but he can't admit it to himself. This is why he's so torn. He's not sure how to deal with it."

"Do you think it's because of Maggie? Is he torn between me and her?" I was on the verge of tears.

"No, not likely. She's forcing her way in, but I don't believe she's part of the equation. His heart yearns for you, and his mind is keeping him emotionally distant. He doesn't think he's worthy of love, and he's afraid of hurting you. And this is why I'm asking you to be patient with him. Give him time to sort out his emotions and get his mind in tune with his heart. He needs to forget his past and love again without fear."

"How can I help him when I don't know about his past? How is he going to sort it out? What if he doesn't?" I shook my head.

"He will, Sabrina. He will. But the museum issues, the economic situation, and the robbery of the jewels are keeping him busy. And his brother's disappearance, along with my poor state of mind . . . I'm afraid it's taking a toll on him. He's my strong boy, the one who always holds the fort and takes care of everything and everyone. But I think this time there's more on his plate than even he can handle. And the last thing he needed was to fall in love."

I looked down to avoid her gaze, feeling miserable and guilty.

"But your presence, despite the unfortunate timing, has made him happy. He's suffering because he doesn't want to hurt you and he doesn't know how to protect you from himself."

It was too much to take. She had told me a lot about Nikos's emotional state. Was she right? How could I help him get through this turmoil when all I wanted was to be with him no matter what? I hugged her, my eyes filling with tears.

"I will do whatever is in my power to be with him and help him, if that's what he wants," I said, nearly choking.

"He needs you, Sabrina, but he doesn't trust his heart yet. I'm sorry to burden you with it. I must sound desperate, especially since I just met you. But I want to see my Nikos happy. And please . . ." She tightened her grip on my hands and gave me an imploring look.

"Please don't mention anything to him about this conversation. He wouldn't be happy to know I'm getting involved in his affairs, but this time I can't help it. I haven't seen him like this for a long time. His attitude and his behavior have changed since he met you. For the last three weeks, before you came, he's been restless, lost in his thoughts. And he doesn't understand his feelings. A mother knows her son."

"No, I won't say anything to him." I shook my head. "Thank you for your trust. This explains why he's distant sometimes. It hasn't been easy for me either, Ms. Soulis. Maggie's presence makes me insecure. But I'm in love with Nikos, and if there's any chance to make him happy, I'll fight for it; I promise you."

Ms. Soulis gave me a kiss on the cheek. Taking my arm into hers, she walked me back to the veranda, where Nikos waited for us. He stood up as soon as he saw us.

"I see you two are getting along well."

"Very much so," Ms. Soulis said, taking his arm into hers. As we left the restaurant, the parking attendant gave the car keys back to Nikos. His mother insisted on sitting in the back, so I took the passenger seat next to her son. When we arrived at the hotel, we all got out of the car.

"I hope to see you again before you go back to Houston, my dear." She hugged me and kissed my cheek. "It's been a pleasure to meet you. I hope you have a great time with your museum tour. And if you need anything while you're here, please call me."

She got into the passenger seat I had just vacated.

"I hope you were not bored with your first night in Athens," Nikos said, his finger curling under my chin.

"I couldn't have asked for a better evening. Your mother is adorable. It's been wonderful." I wanted him to kiss me and come upstairs and finish what he had started when he first came into the room. But he had to take his mother home and we'd have to call it a night, to my disappointment. "Will I see you tomorrow?"

He took my hands into his, and my skin tingled with his touch.

"Yes, you will. I have plans for us tomorrow." He kissed my fingers.

"I can't wait to be with you."

"I'll see you soon enough."

He released my hands and got back in the car. The hotel attendant opened the door for me, and I took the elevator up to my room. I had to digest what Ms. Soulis had told me. She wanted me to be patient with Nikos because he was torn. This revelation gave me strength to fight for him.

I wanted to consider the words his mother had said carefully; I wanted to delight in the knowledge that Nikos was in love with me. I knew I couldn't have been wrong all along. I couldn't have been just one more of Nikos's conquests like Jane kept telling me. The way he'd touched me, kissed me, and made love to me must've meant something to him. I'd be a fool if I didn't trust him. And I needed to make sure he would open his heart to me.

Six

I ENTERED THE ROOM, closed the door, and sighed. The smell of Nikos's D&G Light Blue fragrance still lingered in the air. I took my shoes off and placed my purse on the side table. Walking onto the balcony, I looked at the magnificence of the lit monument in front of me. The Acropolis. I'd always wanted to come to this place and meet the Greek god of my dreams, and it was hard to believe it was, in fact, happening. I sat on the lounge chair to enjoy the out-of-this-world view. It reminded me of how much I appreciated Greek culture and mythology. The Parthenon stood majestic. It brought to my mind tales of the gods, their adventures, their naughtiness, their loves and their wars, their human traits of lust, jealousy, and revenge. I was lost in my thoughts. I allowed the time to pass, recounting in my mind some of the love stories of the mischievous Greek gods. I fantasized about Nikos being one of them and wondered what had happened in his past to make him so afraid to love.

"Enjoying the view?"

I jumped out of the chair and looked back. Nikos, in his god-like splendor, was leaning in the doorway of the balcony with his hands resting in his trousers pockets. It seemed he had been there for a while, observing me in silence. I gasped.

"How did you get in here?" I knew it was a stupid question as soon as I asked it. He'd arranged for my room with a view, so it was clear he'd have access to it.

"I told you I'd see you soon." He smiled at me. "We haven't celebrated your arrival yet."

He approached the side table where, a few hours earlier, the hotel attendant had left the bottle of champagne. He popped it open and poured the still-chilled bubbling liquid into the flutes, offering me one. I took it from him, still speechless with his sudden appearance. He raised his in a toast.

"To my beautiful goddess. I hope you have a fantastic time in Greece."

I touched his flute with mine and drank the delicious champagne without taking my eyes off him. He gulped his down, took my empty flute away, and placed both of them back on the table.

Without giving me a chance to do or say anything, his hands wrapped around my waist. He pulled me toward him and kissed me with a demanding intensity. His tongue explored each corner of my mouth with a consuming need, sending a rush of electricity throughout my body, and as he grew with desire, he pulled me even closer. Sliding his hands behind my back to reach the top of my dress, he unzipped it, and it slipped from my body, falling to the floor.

We stepped back into the room toward the bed. I unbuttoned his shirt to caress his ripped torso, and my hands slid down until I touched his clothed arousal. He gazed at me with a smile on his face as he removed his clothes and lay back naked on the bed, pulling me on top of him.

I mounted my Greek stallion and moaned in pleasure as he penetrated me, thrusting deep inside. I rode my Pegasus like a wild nymph as my legs locked around him and I buried my hands in his hair. He gripped both sides of my waist, taking control of the rocking motion of his thrusts, filling me completely. My wetness helped him slide, tight and precise, sending more waves of ecstasy through my shuddering body. I was hot for him. My moans urged him to dive in deeper and faster until the stimulating contractions sent us both on a spiraling release of lust. I whimpered in pleasure, totally satiated. Nikos rolled me gently off him and pinned me down on the bed, kissing me hungrily. As his kisses slowed and he let go, I panted after so much satisfaction.

He got out of bed and stepped onto the balcony. His fingers combed through his hair. He seemed troubled, anxious. I wondered what was going through his mind. Now that I was aware something from his past was bothering him, it was a little easier to understand his behavior. I wrapped myself in one of the bed sheets and followed him, touching his arm.

"Nikos," I whispered. He pulled me closer to him in a tight embrace and kissed my head. "What's bothering you?"

He didn't answer me. Instead, he kissed my head again and shook his own. I leaned my head on his shoulder. *Oh, my Nikos, why don't you open up to me? Why don't you let me in all the way? I can feel your sadness. I can feel your pain. I need to know. I want to help you. I'm here for you. Always.* I wish I could tell him, but I'd never betray his mother. I was going to be patient and understanding until he allowed me into his life with no restraints.

Without warning, he left me and returned to the room. I watched him dress in silence. When he finished buttoning his shirt, he opened his arms and gave me that irresistible smile that made me melt.

"Come here, my goddess."

I walked toward his strong embrace. "Don't worry about me. I have a lot on my mind, but my biggest concern is you."

I hugged him tight. "Why? I'm feeling great. It's been a wonderful night. I can't believe I'm here with you. I thought I'd never see you again."

He cupped my head with both his hands and looked deep into my eyes. Instead of desire, this time his eyes emanated a sadness he wasn't able to hide.

"You told me you could handle this relationship. But it's not been easy on you. I already hurt you. There's no glamour in love, Sabrina, only pain."

"What do you want to tell me? What do you feel for me? Why are you—"

He didn't allow me to finish. His mouth was on mine, kissing me with fiery passion again. I pushed him away, although it hurt me not to be in his arms receiving his kiss.

"Don't just kiss me to avoid my question, Nikos. I need to know. What do you feel?"

He released me and paced around the room, combing his fingers through his hair.

"Don't I show enough? Can't you tell how much I want you?" He lifted his arms, exasperated.

"That you want me, yes." I nodded. "That you want to kiss me and make love to me, yes, you do."

"Isn't it enough? Isn't it what you want?" He stepped out of the room and onto the balcony without looking at me.

I followed him and stood next to him.

"I want you, Nikos. But I want your love, not just your desire and your lust for me." I touched his strong arm, but he didn't move. He stared at the temple of the gods in front of us. After a few seconds of silence, he looked back at me and wrapped his arms around my waist.

"Love hurts, Sabrina. Love is suffering. Love only brings pain. I've seen what it's done to my mother—and to me."

"Why would you say this? Who has hurt you this badly? Why don't you want to take a chance with me?" *Nikos, I need to know. Tell me what made you so afraid to love*, I begged him in my thoughts.

"Love is not something you want to take a chance with. I don't want to take the chance of hurting you, of losing you. I already—" He paused, his eyes penetrating me as if in search of something he'd lost and didn't know if he'd find again. "I care about you, Sabrina, more than I've cared for anyone in a long time. But I'll never forgive myself for allowing this to escalate. I should've stopped myself." His fingers touched my face and traced the lines of my jaw. "You're special, Sabrina, and you deserve much better."

"It's up to me to decide what I deserve. And if you regret having slept with me—"

He interrupted me. "What I regret is allowing myself to hurt you."

"You didn't hurt me, Nikos. I already told you I was willing to take a chance, and I'd rather spend this special time with you than not. No matter what. If I get hurt or heartbroken, it's also a conscious decision on my part. I don't want to argue with you, but I can't stop loving you. All I want right now is to be with you. Please, don't do this to me."

He planted a gentle kiss on my forehead. "I can't stop wanting you, Sabrina. This is a dangerous game." He sighed.

I realized I was pushing him. As much as I wanted him to open up to me, his mother had asked me to be patient, and I'd promised her I would. There was something I didn't know about his past. I had to be careful not to distance him from me further.

"If it's a game, I'll play with fire then," I joked to lighten up the mood.

He shook his head, a faint smile showing on his lips.

"You need some rest, princess. And I have a meeting with the Interpol agents in the morning. They're picking up a possible clue in Cyprus. Such a coincidence after they helped me trace the last movements of my brother. I don't know what his whereabouts have to do with the jewels, though. I hope you sleep well."

"Am I going to see you tomorrow?" I wrapped my arms around his waist.

"Do you want to?" His hands drifted toward my lower back, tickling me lightly.

"I don't have any plans; I'm all yours tomorrow."

"I'll come by around lunch to give you some time to rest."

"Thank you again for an amazing evening, and tell your mother I really enjoyed meeting her. She's a wonderful woman."

"Yes, she is. Thank you for being so understanding with her. She liked you a lot. If you need something, call me. Anytime."

His kiss came fierce and full of desire. Before I knew it, he'd released me and left. I sighed. My troubled Nikos had too much on his plate. But I'd do whatever I must to ease his tension and make him happy. If he'd only let me.

Seven

MULTIPLE KNOCKS ON THE door awakened me. Still drowsy from sleep, I got up and peeked through the peephole to see a cheerful Curt on the other side of the door. I'd forgotten he was in Greece with me. So much had happened in such a short period of time since he'd retired to his room the evening before.

"Good morning, Curt! Please come in. I just woke up." I allowed him into my room.

"Hello, beautiful. Sorry for waking you up. I thought we might have breakfast together at the hotel restaurant overlooking the Acropolis. I haven't seen it yet." He stood by the door.

I opened the curtains and introduced him to the magnificent view of the world-famous monument. "Voilà. You can enjoy it as much as you want while I take a shower and get ready for breakfast."

Curt drifted toward the balcony as if in slow motion, opening his mouth in silent disbelief. He put his hands on his chest and stared for a few seconds at the ruins, speechless.

"Oh . . . my . . . Zeus! How did you get a room with a view? Oh, don't tell me. Don't tell me! It was our Greek god, wasn't it?"

I skipped toward him, giggling like a little girl. He gave me a big hug.

"You lucky goddess." He looked at the champagne flutes on the side table. "And champagne! Oh, my, am I jealous."

I gave him a soft slap on his arm. "Promise to be a good boy, and I'll tell you about it when we go for breakfast."

I got into the shower, leaving Curt at the balcony, feasting his eyes upon the Acropolis.

Soon we made our way to the hotel's rooftop restaurant, where the magical view of the Acropolis welcomed us. The breakfast consisted of eggs, bacon, sausage, grape leaves, and different kinds of pastries. Curt was beside himself with excitement, absorbing the fantastic sight in front of us. It was hard to believe we were in Athens.

"So, how is our marvelous Greek god?" He took a sip of his coffee.

"Busy, to say the least. He's overwhelmed dealing with the theft of the jewels. And the economic situation of the museum. He'll come by during lunchtime to take me out. You should stop by to say hi." I took a bite of one of the delicious pastries I'd filled my plate with.

"I will, yes, thank you. I'd love to see Nikos. I miss working with him in the museum. So sad the internship is over. Maybe I can ask him for a job here. Oh, what a dream!" He laughed, thinking about it. "So you two are together, I suppose? It's not hard to guess when you got a room with a view and a bottle of champagne."

"It's complicated, Curt. But he's incredible. Yes, he got me the room with a view, ordered champagne, and took me to dine in a magnificent Greek restaurant last night. It was the most impressive welcome I've ever had in my life. I never know what to expect from him." I put another spoonful of sugar in my coffee and stirred it. I didn't tell Curt about last night's dinner with Ms. Soulis and what she told me about Nikos. This was a secret I wanted to keep to myself.

"The man is a hopeless romantic. After the bouquet of Persephone he sent you, I have no doubts the god is in love with you."

I sighed. "If things were not so convoluted . . . and there's the distance between us."

"Have hope. It's good to be in love. And with him. Oh, lucky, lucky you. He's all that, isn't he?" he asked with a mischievous grin.

"Curt, you bad boy. Yes, he's all that and much more."

When we finished breakfast, we decided to take a stroll in the surrounding area. We wanted to explore the Pláka, known as the "Neighborhood of the Gods" due to its proximity to the Acropolis. The old historical neighborhood of Athens was within walking distance of the hotel. We strolled along the streets, admiring the sounds, colors, scents, and neoclassical architecture.

After about two hours exploring the Pláka, taking pictures, and shopping for souvenirs, we returned to the hotel. Nikos was standing by the reception. As usual, my body reacted when I laid my eyes upon him. Dressed in a white polo shirt and jeans, his sunglasses resting on top of his head, he looked like the cover model of a man's fashion magazine. I'd never get over how stunning he was. With shaking legs and sweaty palms, I approached him, and Curt followed me.

"I'm so happy to see you, Nikos," Curt said. "You look fabulous."

"How have you been, Curt? How were the last days of the internship?" Nikos opened his arms to hug me. I wasn't expecting him to show any kind of intimacy between us in public. I blushed before placing myself in the comfort of his strong embrace. Curt's eyes widened, stunned to see Nikos acting so warm toward me in his presence. Nikos seemed to be in better spirits than he had been last night, and there were no visible signs of his troubled mind.

"Oh, we miss you so much at the museum, Nikos. Working with you was the best thing that has ever happened to me on a professional level. See what it got me? A week in Athens with Dr. Gould. I can't thank you enough for all you taught me when you were in Houston. You're the best."

Nikos bowed his head. "Thank you, Curt. It's been my pleasure to work with you, too. If you need any letters of recommendation, please don't hesitate to ask me. You two are the best students I've ever met." He kissed my head and ran his fingers beneath my hair up the back of my neck, causing me to shudder. He wasn't hiding our relationship from Curt.

"Would you care to join us for lunch?" Nikos asked Curt.

"Oh, no, thank you. It's nice of you to ask, but we just came back from walking around the Pláka. I want to rest for a while before meeting with Dr. Gould and the guests for lunch a little later. Besides, I need to catch up with Robert back home. The time difference is too complicated. You two should enjoy your day." Curt chuckled and winked at me.

"It's nice to see you, Curt. If Dr. Gould brings you guys to the museum, please come see me."

Curt nodded and smiled before heading toward the elevator.

Niko faced me. "What about you, goddess? Did you sleep well?"

"I'd have slept better if you'd been by my side." Blood rushed to my cheeks from the intensity of his look.

His lips touched mine. "Shall we go to lunch? I'm starving."

As he took my hand, he led me out of the hotel and into the busy streets of Athens. After about five minutes, we stopped in front of an old-looking building. He opened the door for me, and I entered an elegant, quiet, cozy restaurant. The maitre d' rushed immediately toward us.

"Herete, Dr. Soulis," he said to Nikos, then turned to me and bowed. "Herete, Miss. Welcome to Mani Mani."

"Efharisto," I responded, attempting to practice the Greek words I was learning. The friendly man took us to an inviting table in the corner. It was a most romantic setting. After offering us menus, he excused himself. A waiter came and filled our glasses with fresh, cold water.

"This restaurant serves traditional Peloponnesian cuisine, and it's one of my local favorites. I hope you enjoy it," Nikos said in his exotic accent. "Should I order for you?"

I looked at the menu. There were so many choices. "I'm afraid so. Yes, please order for me."

Nikos chuckled. "I'll get you one of my favorite dishes."

He reached for my hands, keeping his hypnotic eyes on mine. Blood was rushing to my cheeks again. The power this man exerted over me was beyond my control. He sucked lightly on my fingers, sending shocks of desire through my body. As I let out a whimper and pulled my hand back from him, he showed me his to-die-for smile and winked. Absolutely irresistible.

The maitre d' returned with a bottle of wine and explained in broken English that it was made from a fragrant Greek red-wine grape variety, Aghiorghitiko. It was also called St. George, which would be easier for me to pronounce. He offered a taste to Nikos, and after degusting the wine, Nikos gave an approving nod. After filling our glasses, the maitre d' took our order. I had no idea what Nikos had ordered for me since they were speaking Greek.

Nikos raised his glass toward me for a toast. "I'm glad I can share this moment with you."

"Me too," I whispered before sipping the delicious wine. "Do you come here often?"

"Once in a while. It's one of my favorite restaurants, and I only share it with special people."

Jealousy crept up on me as soon as he said these words. I visualized him bringing Maggie to this restaurant. Or some other woman who might have been special to him. He frowned and tilted his head as if he'd noticed a swift change in my expression. I could swear he was reading my mind.

"What's wrong?"

"Nothing. Nothing, really." I knew better than to mention Maggie. I lowered my face, ashamed of my own ridiculous thoughts.

"I didn't bring Maggie here if that is what you're thinking. I come here often by myself and sometimes I bring my mother with me. It's been a long time since I've come to this restaurant with a . . ." He paused for a second as if he wanted to find the correct word. "A date. Sabrina, I'm here with you now, and I want to savor every minute of it. Don't let the ghost of a rumor get in the way of our moment. It's you and me, nobody in the past, nobody in the future. Just the two of us right here, right now. Don't you want this?"

"Yes, that's all I want." I hated myself for nearly ruining the day. But I was still insecure about him, especially after last night's conversation. I wondered who the date had been if it hadn't been

Maggie. "Nothing feels better in the whole world than to be here with you, Nikos."

The waiter came in bringing the plates, which saved me from the awkward moment I'd created. I had to stop allowing Maggie's shadow to come between us. This wasn't the way to earn his trust and conquer his heart. I had to exercise more self-control and be confident. If he didn't want to be with me, why would he bring me here to one of his favorite restaurants in the first place? I wasn't competing against Maggie. I was competing against my own insecurity.

"Enjoy," the waiter said. He placed on the table a plate of orzo with mushrooms and truffle oil for me and pork tenderloin with figs and honey for Nikos. Both were culinary delicacies. The fruity and spicy red wine complimented their delectable flavors. Nikos had a gourmet flare for food, and I was glad he had ordered for me. I would never have thought orzo with mushrooms would be so tasty. The exotic combination of flavors and aroma just made me hungrier for him.

While we ate, he told me what was going on. His brother's whereabouts in Cyprus intrigued him. The museum had received a ransom note a few days earlier demanding money in exchange for the jewels. Yet the agents hadn't disclosed that information to him until this morning. Mr. Wallendorf had been notified of the ransom note and was ready to make the payment. It was a complicated situation.

They had traced the call somehow to Nikos's brother's phone. They'd also received intel about some unusual activity in Cyprus. Black market art dealers were coming in and out of the island. Nikos wanted to go look for his brother, but the agents had advised against it. As a local archaeologist and a staff member of the renowned museum, his presence might create unnecessary tension.

He was expecting a call from the agents at any time. And he still hadn't gone to Amphipolis to oversee the excavation of the possible tomb of Alexander the Great's epic period. Even though he had so much to deal with, he was there with me, spending precious time to make me feel welcomed and desired. My heart filled with more love and passion for this man who was a hero in his own way. I would be the luckiest woman in the world if I were able to conquer him once and for all.

"I'd love to go to Amphipolis with you," I said. "I wish I could extend my trip for at least one more week."

Nikos leaned closer to the table and rested his chin on his wrist, observing me with caution. "You want to go to Amphipolis with me?" he asked in a serious tone.

I nodded. "Yes. If I can spend another week with you to explore Amphipolis, I'll be in heaven. I've never seen an authentic dig. But I must go back to real life. The classes are waiting, and so are my students." I bit my lower lip in frustration, remembering my dream would be over in less than a week.

"If you want, I'll call Dr. Jones and tell him I'm inviting you to take part in my expedition. I'm sure he'll be able to work something out with the university and your job."

"Are you serious? You think I might?" I stuttered, excited about the possibility to spend another week with him.

"Of course I'm serious. I can make it happen if you want to see Amphipolis." He took my hands into his. "The place is amazing. Seeing it in person will give you a magnificent insight into this historical period."

"Yes, I want to see the site. I want to go with you." I squeezed his hands.

His smile illuminated the whole room. "I'm glad you do. I'll teach you about Greece's archaeology in Amphipolis. I'll place some calls later today and make sure you won't get in trouble with school and work. And don't worry about your ticket. I'll take care of it, too."

There he was, acting like a teacher again, although I didn't want to be his student. But I loved how passionate he was about the career he chose.

"Are you ready to enjoy the rest of the day with me?"

Yes, I'm ready to enjoy the rest of my life with you. "Where are we going?"

"We're taking a road trip to Cape Sounion."

I gasped. "Cape Sounion?" I couldn't hide my excitement.

60

"Didn't you ask me for it?" He winked.

"Yes, but I didn't think we'd have time or that you'd remember." I clasped my hands.

"Your wish is my command. Cape Sounion is about an hour and a half away. I want to make sure we get there early enough to see the Temple of Poseidon when it's still light. Then we'll watch the sunset."

Eight

WE LISTENED TO MUSE and Coldplay, some of our favorite bands, on our way to Cape Sounion, reminding me of our weekend trip to San Antonio. It seemed it had happened such a long time ago instead of only a few weeks back. When *The Scientist* played, Nikos brought me closer to him and held me tight. After all, it was the goodbye song he'd sent me when he left Houston.

Nikos was thrilled that I wanted to go to Amphipolis with him. He told me as much as he knew about the excavation and what they were doing at the site. He was proud of his team and couldn't wait to go there and inspect what was being done in person. He hoped that since Interpol was closing in on the situation with the jewels, he'd be able to leave Athens, as he was looking forward to resuming his routine and normal working life.

After about an hour and a half driving south of Athens, we arrived at the southernmost tip of the Attica peninsula. The area was packed with tour buses and tourists. I thought it was going to be hard to see the Temple of Poseidon with the crowd around. But Nikos showed his museum badge at the entry booth of the temple and we were given immediate access without having to wait in the long line to buy the ticket.

"The perks of being an archaeologist and a museum director in

Greece—open access." He smirked. He held my hand as we climbed to the top of one of Greece's most recognizable temples. The famous temple was set high on a rocky hilltop overlooking the Aegean Sea. It was easy to see why it was one of the most beautiful archaeological sites in the country. The temple that paid homage to Poseidon, the god of the seas, was built around 440 BC with forty-two white marble Doric columns rising twenty feet high. Unfortunately, only fifteen columns remained today. The hall of worship used to house a towering twenty-foot-tall bronze statue of Poseidon; however, it didn't survive the times either. We strolled around the famed ruins, appreciating what was still left of it. The view from the temple was magnificent. I gazed at the glittering sea in bewilderment as Nikos pointed out to me the Peloponnese islands sprouting on the horizon on that beautiful, clear afternoon.

As we stopped by one of the columns, he showed me the inscription of Lord Byron's autograph. Legend had it that when the famous British poet visited Greece he inscribed his name on one of the columns. Even though it's not known for sure if it's indeed his signature, it has been preserved as a testimony to the great poet's travels, adding to the romantic aura of the site.

"Funny how this act of vandalism is cherished because it's from a famous poet." Nikos shook his head.

His cell phone, which had been unusually quiet all day along, buzzed in his jeans pocket. He took it out, looked at the screen, and frowned.

"This is Nikos," he said. I looked away from him to gaze at the beautiful sea in front of me and let him deal with his call. "No," he responded over the phone, "I'm not near the museum now, and I'm not going there. There's nothing to do except wait for the agents to call me tomorrow and brief me on what is going on. You need to be patient." There was another moment of silence as he listened to the caller. Then he continued, his tone growing impatient and agitated. "Yes, my brother might be in Cyprus, but I'm not going there. The agents are taking care of it. They won't need the ransom money until they figure out what's going on. I told you I'll call your father if I have any news. The agents can keep him abreast of the situation better than I can."

I sighed, realizing Nikos was talking to Maggie. I should've guessed she wouldn't leave him alone, especially after threatening me to stay away from her "boyfriend" while I was in Greece. At least the time difference was keeping her at bay for a while. I knew I had to control myself so the call wouldn't interfere with the mood of our romantic outing.

"It's none of your business what I'm doing or who I am with. I'll call you if there are any new developments. And no, there's no need for you to come back here now. I'm not going to be in Athens. I have things to take care of in Amphipolis."

He hung up and placed the phone back in his pocket. I faced him.

"What happened? You sounded upset."

He wrapped his arms around my waist and brought me close to him.

"I'm sure you realized I was talking to Maggie. Don't worry about her. She's restless because of the ransom. Her dad has the money and wants the payment done right away. He doesn't want to jeopardize the fate of the jewels. He also feels responsible for them. But this is beyond my control. I can't overrule what Interpol is doing. They've decided to do a sweep in Cyprus before giving in to the demands of the robbers."

"What would you do if it was up to you?" I tightened my embrace.

"I would run away with you to Crete and disappear in the Minotaur's labyrinth." He gave me a light kiss on the lips. "Come on, we'll find a place to sit and watch the sunset. It's the most beautiful spectacle of all. I want to enjoy this moment with you and not think about anything else."

Holding my hand firmly, he led the way through the ruins until we found a spot at the edge of the hilltop. Nikos sat on the ground and settled me between his legs, wrapping his arms around my waist. Waves of desire swept through me when he kissed the back of my neck and nibbled on my earlobes. A moan escaped my lips, and I turned my face to kiss his mouth. This setting was the most romantic place I'd ever visited, and being with Nikos was beyond incredible. When I looked again at the wonderful scene in front of me, I realized we were not alone. Several people surrounded us, eager to see the amazing sunset.

The sun melted into the mirrored surface of the quiet sea, emanating vivid hues of gold and red. The calm, idyllic water swallowed the ball of fire that struggled to remain afloat. Its reflection radiated triumphantly out of the sea's depth, giving the last surviving rays the glowing ecstasy of its demise. An array of colors that could only be compared to an art museum's masterpiece painted the sky with the precision of a master's brush strokes. It prompted not only gasps, but a long bout of applause from the dazed and overwhelmed spectators.

It had been the most spectacular sunset I'd ever watched. The tourists were getting ready to leave, but Nikos held me in place and didn't move until the site was clear. Dusk was settling in, and the moon was rising, giving a faint and dreamy lighting to this magical place. After a while, Nikos finally got up and led me toward the entry booth. The security guard was preparing to shut down for the night. He approached the man and they exchanged a few words in Greek before Nikos showed him his ID and a badge. I had no idea what he was talking to the man about, but after inspecting Nikos's documents, the guard smiled and shook Nikos's hand with enthusiasm before bowing to me. After saying something else to Nikos, he left.

"Come, let's go back to the temple," Nikos said after the man disappeared down the hill.

I raised my eyebrows.

"I got clearance. I've got authorization to be at any archaeological site in Greece beyond the regular hours of visitation." He held my hand as we climbed the steps back to the temple. Darkness had now descended upon us, except for the beautiful glow of the moon reflected on the serene waters of the mystical Aegean Sea.

"I want you to remember this night."

"I remember all the nights I've ever spent with you, Nikos," I murmured. "How could I forget any minute? Impossible."

When we got to the top, Nikos stopped by one of the temple's columns, facing me. His eyes reflected the moon, shining with desire.

"Tonight, I'll make the gods jealous."

He pinned me against the column and kissed me with passionate hunger. I surrendered at once, opening my mouth to receive his ravenous kiss and burying my fingers in his hair. He softened his kiss until his lips just nibbled on mine. When he lowered his head to nuzzle against my neck, his breathing was heavy. His fingers traced the contour of my shoulders, lifting the straps of my dress. They slid down my arms, baring my upper body. His fingers advanced to my erect nipples, and he pinched them, making me moan.

"Oh, Nikos," I whispered, closing my eyes while my skin tingled, craving his touch. His wet tongue trailed down my neck and came to rest on one of my swollen nipples. He took it into his mouth and sucked while his fingers drew circles around the other. I clawed at his hair, unable to contain the desire sweeping through me. After stroking both my nipples with his tongue, he moved down. His lips brushed lightly at my skin and aroused me as only he could.

He crouched down to lift my skirt, and his moist lips traced the curve of my hips. His tongue swirled across my navel, licking me and kissing me so tenderly my legs shook. He removed the lacy panties I wore, and as he pushed my thighs apart, the swipe of his tongue touched my most sensitive skin. I throbbed with yearning as Nikos sucked and licked me with a steady rhythm; a rush of heat spread through my groin. Just as I was about to explode in ecstasy, he slid his finger inside me. I gasped, arching my back against the column, absolutely ready to receive him. This was torture.

"You're ready for me, goddess," he whispered as he stood up and lifted my hips to enter me. He slid inside of me, making me moan with pleasure. Wrapping me in his embrace to soften the impact of his thrusts on my back against the column, he kissed me with hunger. With every heavy breath, his thrusts increased in intensity as my legs locked around him, imprisoning him within me more tightly. He filled me completely. For a fraction of a second, I opened my eyes to peek at the sea beyond Nikos—the only witness to the bliss that followed when I couldn't stand the pleasure any longer and screamed as Nikos relieved his sexual tension in perfect timing with my own.

He lay on the grass, bringing me down to rest on his shoulder. We gazed at the beautiful starry sky. The faint illumination of the moon gave it an eerie yet romantic look. I wanted to melt into him and never be apart again. I loved him so much it hurt, but I was afraid to tell him. I didn't want to scare him away from me when he hadn't been able to open up about his own feelings. I had to be patient, but until when? How long would I have to wait for him to sort them out, as his mother had asked?

"I told you the gods were going to be jealous of me. I've just made love to the most beautiful goddess of all." He kissed my forehead.

I caressed his toned torso. "This is unforgettable, Nikos. This place, this magical place, you, and how much I . . ." I paused, afraid of my own words.

"How much what?"

"How much I want to be with you." The words I wanted to say wouldn't come out. *How much I love you, Nikos! Can't you tell how much I love you?* He held me tightly and kissed my hair. I didn't say anything else. I didn't want to destroy the romantic appeal of the night with the what-ifs of our situation, with declaring my endless love, with asking him what I meant to him. Would he open up to me now that we were in this idyllic place? Was it only lust? Would he love me the same as I loved him?

His grip tightened around me. "I've dreamt about being here with you. Tonight, you're mine, and the gods are our only witnesses."

"I want to love you." I got on top of him. He stared at me with desire in his eyes and kissed me as if the night was about to end. I touched his broad torso, feeling the firmness of his muscles, and released his kiss, allowing my mouth to explore every inch of his soft and fragrant skin. My tongue swirled around his erect nipples while my hand searched for him. He pulsated under my touch, and his body hardened with pleasure. My tongue roamed down his body while my fingers closed firmly around his hardness. I opened my mouth to receive his length and worked my tongue up and down, closing my lips tightly, savoring his delicious salty taste as I gave him pleasure. Suddenly, he pulled me up, turning me so he was on top and thrusting into me like a wild animal.

"You drive me crazy," he whispered as he once again filled me.

We made passionate love on the grounds of the temple again, witnessed only by the gods hidden among the stars above. There was no before and no after; all I knew was I was his and would be his forever. I'd never love anyone else as much as I loved Nikos. I knew it then, at that special moment when we were united as one soul. My love for him was such that I'd do anything for him. When our bodies synchronized in an emotional turbulence of desperate longing and perfect completion, I believed his love, I suffered his pain, I sensed his fear. I understood his struggle against a force he couldn't resist. And I'd do anything to make him happy. Even it if meant sacrificing it all.

He was inside of me, hard, throbbing, pulsating with passionate urgency, making me entirely his, taking control of my movements until we once again came together, satiating our most inner feelings and yearnings for each other. Waiting for our hearts to resume their normal beat, we held each other in silence. This was a magical place, where we'd made love with the blessing of Poseidon. Nothing would ever compare to this night.

"We should get going, goddess," Nikos whispered, breaking the silence. "You have a full day tomorrow with the tour group, and I'm sure I'll be as busy."

I nodded. It was getting late. I had no idea what time it was, and we still had to travel back to Athens. We got dressed, walked around the temple again holding hands, and kissed by the cliff before heading down to the car. If I could make the world stop turning right then and there, I'd have done it to be with him forever in Cape Sounion.

We drove back to Athens without talking much, and I knew I wouldn't see much of him for the rest of the week. If there was a way to extend my trip and go to Amphipolis with him, I'd be the happiest woman alive.

I rested my head on his shoulder, thinking how wonderful this night had been. He turned the music on, and as had become a pattern for us whenever we were together, a sad, beautiful love song was playing. The melancholy voice of Eddie Vedder implored his lover to stay with him, asking her if he'd said he needed her, if he'd said he wanted her, and if he hadn't, what a fool he was. Nikos gave a deep sigh.

"Just breathe," he repeated along with the lyrics.

I nodded, my head still resting on his shoulder. He tapped his fingers on the wheel, following the rhythm of the song, and sang it in a whisper. I closed my eyes, absorbing the lyrics and listening to Nikos's voice. He sounded sad, imitating the singer's tone as someone inundated with sorrow and lost in love.

"No one knows this more than me."

I bit my lower lip. *Are you coming clean with your feelings for me? Are you revealing to me your love through the song?* Was this one of the ways Nikos tried to express himself, through love songs? He'd sing or send me songs whose lyrics had some meaning to us, but he wouldn't say it in his own words to me. *Yes, you told me you needed me; yes you told me you wanted me. Now tell me you love me.*

"What are you doing to me, my princess?" As the music ended, he kissed my head.

"I'm trying to melt the ice wall around your heart," I whispered.

He reached for my hand and squeezed it. "According to my mother, you're succeeding."

"And according to you?"

He brought my hand to his lips and kissed it, keeping his eyes on the road. After a few seconds of silence that seemed too long, a heavy sigh escaped his mouth.

"It's possible," he said, holding my hand tighter.

I was pleased and feeling like a winner. He was finally breaking down and giving me a glimpse of his feelings, thanks to the gods of Olympus. But how much longer would I have to be patient?

Nine

BACK AT THE HOTEL, Nikos accompanied me to my room. As soon as he closed the door behind him, he pulled me to him and kissed me again. I wrapped my arms around his neck. I was fully smitten with this man.

"Are you going to be okay? You need to have a good night's rest; the jet lag's still bothering you," he said, pulling away from the kiss.

I nodded. "Yes, I do need to rest for tomorrow. But each minute spent with you today was worth it."

His phone buzzed in his pocket, and he released me to answer it. The conversation was brief and in Greek, but it sounded tense.

He put the phone back in his pocket and paced around the room. "It was my mother. One of the inspectors called her asking more information about my brother. It's unusual for them to call on a Sunday evening, and she's nervous. I don't want to tell her about the possible link between my brother and what's going on in Cyprus."

"Would they tell her?"

"I hope not. They were questioning her about his friends, if she knew who he was going out with during the last few weeks before he took off." He stopped by the balcony, looking out at the beautiful night.

"Why don't they call you instead of bothering her?"

"I wasn't in the country when they began to investigate. And my brother lives with her, so they assumed she'd be more involved in his activities and his friends. But it's not the case. My brother has gotten mixed up with the wrong sort before, and I have no idea what he's been up to. The whole situation worries me." He opened the door to the balcony and stepped outside, staring at the Acropolis in front of us. After a few seconds, he turned to me and opened his arms, inviting me in. "Come here."

I threw myself into his open arms as he embraced me with tenderness.

"I wish you were here during a time I didn't have to be so caught up with work and all this mess. You may not be able to reach me tomorrow, but don't worry. I'll contact you as soon as I can." His fingers trailed up and down my back.

"I'll be anxiously awaiting your call."

"Focus on your work. Don't think about me." He caressed my face with the back of his fingers.

I closed my eyes, feeling my skin tingle with his touch.

"Promise me you'll give one hundred percent to whatever you do tomorrow. I don't want you to get distracted because of me. This is important for you."

Always the teacher, always the professional.

"Yes, of course, I'll do my best. I'm looking forward to it. I won't disappoint Dr. Jones. Or you." He gave me a quick peck on the lips and stepped back into the room, heading toward the door.

"Nikos," I called after him.

He turned around and faced me, raising his eyebrows.

"I . . . I . . ." *I love you.* The words didn't leave my thoughts. "Thank you for today. It was unforgettable."

His disarming smile spread across his face. "It was my pleasure, goddess." He winked at me and left the room.

I had a hard time falling asleep. My mind played back the whole day spent with Nikos, especially when we were at the Temple of Poseidon. He had been so thoughtful and careful in his planning. When I mentioned to him I'd like to see Cape Sounion, I'd never thought he'd remember it and take me there. Not only to see the temple and the spectacular view, but to experience the sunset and make love in that mystical place. He had outdone himself. Even if he'd had no intentions of impressing me, he'd succeeded in leaving me even more infatuated. Was he even real? He was showing so much love, so much passion, and so much care for me, but he wouldn't admit it. Was he in love with me? What bothered him so much? Why was he so traumatized about letting go? Why wouldn't he delve into his emotions without restraint? *Just breathe,* I told myself, remembering the song we'd just heard in the car.

In the morning, I met Curt at the rooftop restaurant. Dr. Gould and the rest of the group were already there having breakfast before we headed out to our first day of the guided tour.

"You're glowing, doll. How was your day with our hot archaeologist?" Curt asked after giving me a quick hug. I filled my plate with delicious Greek pastries and waited for the waiter to bring me coffee.

"Cape Sounion," I said.

Curt's eyes popped out of his head, and his mouth dropped open as if in a silent scream.

"Complete with sunset," I teased.

"You got to be kidding me! You lucky, lucky girl. You know I love you, don't you? This is the most romantic setting . . . Oh, my! This is beyond all expectations. I'm speechless."

I chuckled. "Yes, talk about expectations. Curt, this man is a dream. Sometimes I have to pinch myself to figure out if I'm dreaming or if he's real. It was without a doubt the best day of my life. It was unforgettable, unbelievable. Unreal."

"He is real, my sweetie, and oh, glorious Zeus, he's so real. I'd love to be living this fairy tale. He's a prince. Wait, no, not a prince—a god, of course. Nikos is a real god from Olympus." He waved his arm around to point at the magnificent view of the Acropolis.

"Did you hear from the guys back home?" I changed the subject.

"Yes, I talked to Robert yesterday. Oh, and there's something I must tell you. Not good news, though."

I frowned, wondering what kind of bad news Robert had given Curt that could affect me far from home.

"Robert found out Maggie is coming back here this week, either tomorrow or the day after."

I shook my head and gritted my teeth.

"Yes, that's how I thought you'd react," he said.

"Why? Why is she coming back here? He told her she didn't need to." I put the pastry I was about to take a bite of back on the plate.

"Nikos told her not to come?"

"Yes. She called him yesterday while he was with me in Cape Sounion. She wanted to come and bring the ransom money." I took a sip of the coffee the waiter had poured for me.

"So that's the issue. She knows he's spending time with you. Or she suspects it and she's definitely not a happy camper. Robert saw her at a party last night, and she was grilling him with questions about what we were doing. Then she said the only reason you agreed to come was because you wanted to seduce her boyfriend."

"I can't believe her. When is she going to stop this? Nikos is *not* her boyfriend. I heard him telling her on the phone not to come and that it was none of her business what he was doing or who he was with. She's coming to haunt him."

"That's for sure." Curt shrugged. "Don't let her intimidate you. Remember, Greek god wants *you*, not her. I don't think she's been to the Temple of Poseidon to watch the sunset with him." He gave a loud laugh.

But the atmosphere had already changed. It annoyed me to know she'd be in Athens when I was trying so hard to make the most out of my limited time with Nikos. And with her around, he'd be even busier and probably in a sour mood.

Dr. Gould came to our table to greet us and briefed us about our program for the day before we headed out with the group. We were starting the tour on the other side of the street to visit the Acropolis and the temples in the area. I was ready and looking forward to it, but the thought of Maggie's impending arrival in Athens overshadowed my excitement. I had to be strong and maintain my professionalism as I couldn't allow these thoughts to take control of my mood. So I gathered my group to chat about the gods of Olympus as we left the restaurant and headed out of the hotel.

The day went by faster than I'd anticipated. By the time we got back, after dining with the group in a cozy local restaurant, I was exhausted from the sightseeing and from playing tour guide. It had been exhilarating to visit the temples with the museum members. They were as interested in Greek mythology and archaeology as I was. And I'd been able to answer their questions and quench their curiosity about the history of Athens and the Acropolis. After all, it was my main interest of study. I had plenty of knowledge from my years in college to teach what I'd learned.

After taking a nice, hot shower, I checked for messages, but there was nothing from Nikos. I wondered how his day had been and if he knew Maggie was coming, but I didn't want to trouble him with it. As I was drifting off to sleep, my phone rang, and I answered with a drowsy voice.

"Hello."

"Did I wake you up?" Nikos's raspy, grave voice made me sit up in bed right away. *Oh, thank God you're calling me, my love. I was so eager to hear from you.*

"No, I've been dreaming about you. I wanted to call you, but I didn't want to bother you."

"You never bother me, Sabrina. You can call me at any time. I may not be able to answer, but you can always leave a message, especially if you need me. How was your day?"

"Satisfying but exhausting. We toured the Acropolis and the temples in the area. I think I did pretty well as a tour guide." I was eager to tell him about my day.

"I'm sure you did. I believe in you. You're a great student, and I knew you'd be perfect for this. Anyhow, I wanted to check on you and see how you're doing."

"Thanks, I'm doing what I can. What about you? Did you hear any news about your brother or the jewels?" I switched the cell phone to my other ear.

"Unfortunately, yes. I don't have much time to tell you all that's going on, but I'm flying to Cyprus in the morning."

"Cyprus?" I covered my mouth with my hand when I realized the question had come out as a scream. I tried to calm down and speak in a normal tone. "You're going to Cyprus tomorrow? When are you coming back?"

"Either tomorrow night or early the next day. The Interpol agents found the jewels. They need a team of experts to ensure they are handled properly and there's nothing missing or damaged before transporting them back to Athens. But there's still another complication." He paused.

With his hesitation, I spoke up. "I know. Curt heard Maggie's on her way. She'll be here sometime soon."

Nikos didn't say anything for a few seconds, and then I heard a loud sigh. "That's not what I was talking about, but thanks for the heads up. I had no idea she was coming. I asked her not to, but it makes no difference. I'll have to deal with it when she gets here."

"I thought you knew." I'd gotten the impression he'd been referring to Maggie when he'd mentioned another complication.

"Sabrina, this is not going to be an easy week. You won't get to see me much, but I want you to know I can't stop thinking about you. I've told Dr. Jones I plan take you to Amphipolis with me next week, and he thinks it's a great idea. If nothing else happens to make my life more convoluted before then, we should have a good time there. But right now, it's quite impossible to have some time together."

"I understand," I murmured. "What were you going to tell me?"

"It's about my brother. He was somehow involved with the heist."

His words came as a blow. I thought about his beautiful, sensitive mother who didn't need to endure such suffering.

"How? Oh my God, does your mom know? Is she okay?"

"Yes. She's aware. The inspectors were at her house for most of the day. She's devastated but holding on. At least we know where he is now, and the authorities will be bringing him back. He's already in custody."

"I'm so sorry to hear this. I'm sorry for your mom. Tell her I'm thinking about her. If she needs my company while you're in Cyprus, I'll come visit her when I'm done with work tomorrow evening." It was the least I could do.

"That's nice of you, and I'm sure she'd appreciate it. But you need to stay with the group and focus on your work. Don't get distracted with my problems."

"Nikos, whatever happens to you concerns me, too. I care about you, and I want to be involved. I don't want you to go through this by yourself. I'm here, I'm here for you. And don't worry about my obligations. I'll take care of what I need to."

"Thank you, Sabrina. I do need you. Your presence here is helping me in more ways than you can imagine."

"Nikos, you're strong and you can handle a lot, but please share with me. I'll be by your side. I'll always be here for you." *I love you. I love you more than anything. You need to know I love you. You need to know I'll do anything for you. You need to know you can trust me.* Why couldn't I just tell him that?

"I'll text you to let you know when I'll be back in Athens."

"Please do. Be careful and have a safe trip."

"I will. Enjoy the city with your guests. I'll see you soon." He hung up.

I'll be missing you like crazy, my love. I'll be thinking about you every second of every day until I hear from you.

What a crazy situation. His brother, of all people, helped steal the jewels. I hoped it wouldn't cause problems for Nikos with the museum. I wondered how his mother was feeling as I realized how critical the whole situation was. It was such bad luck I ended up in Athens during the worst week of the year for Nikos. And to top it off, Maggie was coming to make matters even more difficult. What else could go wrong during my stay in Greece?

Ten

CURT WAS THERE FOR me like the angel he looked like, reminding me to focus on the tour. He proved to be the most loyal friend I could have asked for. We'd always been good friends, but his adulation of Nikos prompted him to behave as my protector when his idol was not around. And I needed this kind of brotherly love next to me. I was doing something I loved, in a country I'd always wanted to visit, and with people I enjoyed. But whatever was happening was affecting me, and I was getting distracted with the situation.

Nikos sent me a text in the evening warning me he had to spend the night in Cyprus. There had been delays, but he'd be back the next afternoon. He hadn't been able to see his brother because the authorities had already taken him back to Athens. I texted him back telling him I'd love to talk to his mother, and he sent me her phone number. I dialed it as soon as I got it.

"Yasa?" The voice on the other side was fragile, weak, and anxious.

"Ms. Soulis? This is Sabrina."

She switched to English. "Oh, hello, my sweet girl. How are you?"

"I'm fine, thanks. Nikos told me about his brother, and I'm sorry to hear it. I wanted to find out how you're doing."

"That's so kind of you, Sabrina. Thank you for thinking about me.

Yes, it's been devastating to know my Yannis had something to do with this horrible incident. I had no idea he'd be willing to jeopardize his brother's job and career by getting together with criminals to rob the museum." Her voice was failing her as if she was about to cry.

"Have you talked to him to confirm?"

"No, I haven't seen him yet. This is just what the inspectors told us. I'll be able to visit with him tomorrow. He's being questioned. Oh, Sabrina, this is such an awful situation."

"If you need me to be with you tonight, I can keep you company," I offered.

"Thank you so much; you're an angel, but I won't bother you. Nikos told me how busy you are. You need to rest, and I'm sure you have another full day of work tomorrow. I'm sorry this has been a less than ideal time for you to be in Athens and spend time with Nikos. Is he treating you well?" she asked.

"Your son is wonderful, Ms. Soulis. I . . . I love him, but I'm afraid to tell it to him. I don't think he's ready to hear it."

I can't believe I just confessed my feelings to her like that.

"If you love him, Sabrina, and I hope you do, please be patient with him. I've asked you this before, and although you don't understand him yet, I'm sure he'll open up to you. I know he's in love with you, but he's torn. You can turn things around for him with your love. He needs you." Her soothing voice comforted me.

"I do love him, Ms. Soulis. And I'll be patient, I promise you. I need him, too. Thank you again for your trust in me. Please call me if I can help. It'd be a pleasure for me to come by and be there for you."

"I appreciate your thoughtfulness, my dear Sabrina. Thank you so much for your call and your concern. Meeting you has been refreshing in the midst of this turmoil."

I sighed as we hung up, thinking how strong she was to ask about me and my relationship with Nikos when she was in so much pain. Nikos was like her. Even in the middle of a crisis, he maintained a calculated calm, as if nothing affected him. I was sure Ms. Soulis had been like him when she was younger. The poor woman didn't need this kind of aggravation in her life, and I felt sorry for her. She'd been abandoned by her husband years ago, had raised her two children by herself, and had sacrificed so much. It was unfair that one of her sons ended up involved with the wrong people, making her suffer more. I ached for Nikos. I wanted to be with him and soothe him in any way I could.

The following day, we visited more fascinating locations with the group. I was learning as much as I was teaching. Visiting those monuments and lecturing about them was, indeed, an unforgettable experience. I knew this opportunity would open many doors for me once I started my job search after getting my master's degree. And visiting the excavation site in Amphipolis would be, professionally speaking, the cherry atop the sundae. Nikos was right—I had to be the best I could. Upon my graduation next summer, my resume would look terrific with all these experiences.

In the evening, Curt and I had dinner in one of the Pláka's restaurants. I hadn't heard from Nikos yet. We chose a cozy, typical restaurant buzzing with tourists. Curt ordered us a bottle of ouzo.

"Drink, girlfriend. I think you need a drink before I tell you the news." Curt poured me a glass.

"Well, if you're going to tell me about Maggie, I don't need a drink. You already told me. And by the way, Nikos had no idea about it. He sounded surprised when I told him she was coming."

"I saw her at the hotel before meeting you in the lobby. She arrived today."

He was right. I needed a drink. I gulped the ouzo without blinking. "Did you talk to her?"

"Of course I did. She asked where you were. I think she had already heard Nikos was out of town but wanted to make sure he wasn't with you."

I bit my lower lip. "I can't believe she's in the same hotel we are. And she's already inquiring about me? She's going to ruin it all for me." I filled my glass and gulped down another shot of ouzo.

Curt immediately took the glass from me. "You're not getting drunk. Not here, and not because of Maggie. You already got drunk once because of this woman, and she's not worth it. Don't let her ruin anything. Greek god wants *you*, not her. He'll have to deal with her."

"I hate it when she talks so possessively of him, as if he were hers. I can't help it, Curt. But you're right. I won't let her ruin the rest of my stay here." My phone buzzed, and I answered right away. "Hello?"

"Hello, goddess. How are you?" My Nikos. His low-pitched voice made me melt.

Curt's eyebrows arched. I covered the phone and whispered to him, "It's Nikos."

He zipped his mouth shut with his fingers, signaling he was going to be quiet. I turned my attention back to Nikos. "Are you back?"

"Yes. I just got home. I'm going to see my mother in a bit. I wanted to talk to you before I head over."

"I talked to your mom yesterday. She's a strong woman, but she's suffering."

"Yes, thanks for calling her. You made her day. I have a lot to tell you, but I don't have time tonight. I wanted to tell you I was back and I want to see you tomorrow night. Do you have any plans?"

"No, there aren't any activities tomorrow evening."

"Okay, then. I'll come to the hotel around seven. I have to go to the museum during the day, and I have meetings with the agents in the afternoon. It's going to be a stressful day, but spending the evening with you will be my reward."

"I can't wait to see you, Nikos. Say hi to your mom for me when you see her."

"I will. See you tomorrow, then." I stared at the phone as it went silent, hoping Nikos would materialize in front of me as though by magic.

Curt's voice broke the spell. "So?"

"I should've told him Maggie's already here," I mumbled.

"I'm glad you didn't. Don't talk to him about Maggie. He called you to ask about *you*, not her, right?" He touched my arm lightly.

"Oh, Curt, what would I do without you?" We giggled.

After dinner, Curt came up to my room, and we studied the

material we had to memorize for the tour. A visit to the museum had been planned for the next morning, and I was sure Dr. Gould would look for Nikos. I realized I hadn't been to the museum yet. Actually, I hadn't seen Nikos's work place or his home. How weird. Most of our interactions had taken place in the hotel, and he was always the one coming over to be with me or pick me up to go somewhere. He'd never mentioned anything about his place, although I knew he didn't live with his mother.

In the morning, the tour bus took us to the world-famous National Archaeological Museum. During the ride, I kept fidgeting with my badge, and by the time we got to our destination, I'd almost broken the plastic wrapper around it.

Dr. Gould distributed the museum tickets and divided the group into three. We spent about an hour and a half browsing the Mythology hall with each of our groups, and then we met at the coffee shop. While our guests rested and had refreshments, Dr. Gould invited us to look for Nikos's office to say hi to him while we had a free minute. Dr. Gould had been to the museum many times before and was fairly familiar with the layout of the staff-only areas. We came to a more isolated aisle of the Sculptures Collection, which lead to a hallway. There were several closed doors, each with a sign written in Greek.

"I can't remember which one is his office." Dr. Gould read the signs on each door in search of Nikos's name. As she searched, one of the doors opened, and Nikos stepped out, dressed in an elegant light-brown three-piece suit that made me gasp. Maggie followed him out of the office. She was wearing a dazzling red dress with matching stilettos, and her beautiful blonde hair cascaded down her face as if she'd just come out of a hair salon. I froze midstep, feeling the blood drain from my face. My legs shook.

"Dr. Soulis!" Dr. Gould exclaimed. "I was looking for you. I came to pay you a quick visit while we're touring the museum."

I noticed Nikos's troubled expression as he faced the three of us. But he was quick to collect himself, extending his hand to Dr. Gould in greeting.

"Hello, Dr. Gould. What a pleasant surprise. I heard you were in town, and I wondered when you'd be visiting the museum." He glanced at me.

Maggie remained still behind him, her eyes piercing through me.

"You remember Curt and Sabrina from the museum, right?" Dr. Gould waved her hand toward us.

Nikos bowed to me and Curt, smiling courteously. "Yes, of course I remember them, Dr. Gould. Two brilliant students are not easy to forget."

Dr. Gould turned to Maggie. "Maggie! You look marvelous. I didn't know you were in Athens. How nice to see you here. I hope your father's doing well."

Maggie shook Dr. Gould's hand and seemed to force a smile. It was obvious she wasn't excited to bump into us.

"It's nice to see you, too, Dr. Gould. My father's doing great, thank you. He's put me in charge of Nikos's affairs as it relates to the jewels and future exhibits he'll be sponsoring. We have a lot of work to do."

She just had to rub my face in the fact she was able to work with Nikos.

"I bet you do," Dr. Gould replied. "And it's so noble of your father to sponsor the arts. I'm glad you're helping Nikos in his quest to improve the financial outlook of this magnificent museum. The world would lose so much if this place closed its doors."

Maggie's eyes shot a mean look at me before scanning me from head to toe. Then she threw her arms around Nikos unexpectedly, securing him in a tight embrace.

"Nikos is wonderful, and it's my pleasure to help him, Dr. Gould. Together, we're accomplishing great things."

Nikos didn't do anything to return her affection. He closed his eyes while his mouth locked up in a thin line. I was sure he was caught off guard by her unexpected embrace. Maggie was testing his patience. When he opened his eyes again, he looked furious for a second before regaining his usual cool. He freed himself subtly from Maggie's grasp and held her wrist with a strong grip. She tried to pull her arm free without calling too much attention to the movement, but he held onto her firmly. I wasn't sure if Dr. Gould had noticed, but Nikos was definitely trying to avoid a scene with her.

"Dr. Gould, it's a shame you came to see me at such an unfortunate time. I wish I had time to sit down and chat with you three while you're here visiting. But Maggie just arrived from Houston and we're on our way to a meeting with the museum director. I'm sorry we have to leave you."

While still holding Maggie's wrist, he extended his other hand to Dr. Gould.

"I understand, Dr. Soulis." She shook his hand. "And I'm glad we got to see you, even if for a brief moment. We look forward to welcoming you back to Houston. I hope you work things out here and grace us with your presence soon. Good luck. Bye, Maggie, I'll see you in Houston. Say hello to your father for me."

Maggie nodded but didn't say anything. Nikos turned to me and Curt.

"Sabrina, Curt, enjoy your stay in Athens. This is a great opportunity for you."

He bowed again. This time, his dark, expressive eyes caught mine for a moment longer before he walked down the hallway, dragging Maggie by the wrist.

"Oh, it's a shame he's so busy," Dr. Gould said. "I'd have loved to chat with him about what's going on. Let's head back to our guests, then. By the way, don't they look great together? I hope they work things out—such a wonderful couple. I think they complement each other well."

I swallowed hard. That was the last thing I wanted to hear—that Nikos and Maggie looked good together.

"What a shame Dr. Soulis was not available. It was great seeing him, anyhow." Curt came to the rescue and diffused the conversation. I was relieved he did, so Dr. Gould wouldn't notice my sour expression.

As the butterflies fluttered in my stomach and my heart pounded uncontrollably, my mind raced with thoughts of Maggie and Nikos together again. She looked gorgeous and so did he. And as much as I hated to admit it, Dr. Gould was right—their looks complemented each other. Not their personalities, though.

"How are you feeling?" Curt pulled me to the side when we got back to the coffee shop. "Her behavior shouldn't bother you."

"It's so damn hard to see them together, Curt. I can't help it." I looked down, shaking my head.

"She is provoking you, trying to establish her territory. It was obvious Nikos was uncomfortable when she threw herself at him. But she did it because you were there. Keep your cool."

I sighed. "I'll do my best. Thanks for being here for me. Your support means the world."

He opened his arms to engulf me in a protective embrace. "You're my sister, baby girl. You can count on me."

Eleven

I HAD NO IDEA how the rest of Nikos's day passed. At least he was coming to see me in the evening, so as soon as we got back to the hotel, I prepared a nice, soothing bath. It was what I needed to relax and get ready for another night of love with my Greek god. I didn't want to think about Maggie's presence, the jewels, or his brother's interrogation. I wanted us to love each other without restraint.

A knock at the door surprised me. The clock by the bed read 6:40 p.m. Nikos was early, and I wondered why he hadn't just opened the door since he had a key. I wrapped myself in the plush hotel bathrobe and opened the door, a big smile spread across my face.

"Hello, Sabrina."

Maggie stood in front of me, frowning. She stepped inside the room and closed the door behind her, making me take a few steps back. I nearly stumbled as I stared at her in disbelief, my smile turning into a scowl.

"Not who ou were expecting?"

"What do you want, Maggie? I have nothing to talk to you about." I was furious with her petulance. The last thing I wanted was a confrontation with her before Nikos arrived.

"Oh, but you do." She advanced toward the balcony and opened the curtains. The astonishing Acropolis came into view. "You have a lot to tell me. Explain this." She waved at the beautiful monument.

I gritted my teeth. She was out of line. Absolutely insane.

"I have no idea what you're talking about. I have nothing to explain to you. You need to leave."

"Did Nikos get this room for you? Because you know, it's not easy to get this prime view unless you're a regular customer. And you're not. What are you doing to him, you whore? I told you Nikos is mine."

She put her hands on her waist, probably to intimidate me, waiting for me to make a move.

"Maggie, get out of my room. I owe you no explanation about my relationship with Nikos. You don't own him."

My voice came out calmer than I expected. I needed to be strong and get Maggie out of my room without a scandal. She paced around and stared at the balcony again. Then she looked at me with the same outraged expression.

"I'll make your life miserable, Sabrina. Mark my words. Who do you think you are? You pitiful bitch. You have no chance against me. Nikos is screwing you because you're throwing yourself at him. You think he loves you? You think he wants you? Think again."

Her words were poison. I pointed at the door.

"You need to leave. Now. I won't listen to you offend me in my own room. Get out before I call security."

"You wouldn't dare. You need to leave Nikos alone. Stop chasing him, once and for all."

The door opened, and Nikos stepped inside. He froze as soon as he saw Maggie standing on the balcony. My heart jumped out of my chest, and I heard Maggie gasp. The color left her face. She looked like a ghost.

"You have the key to her room?" She pointed at me threateningly.

Nikos frowned. "What are you doing here?" His voice was monotone and serious. However, instead of waiting for her to respond, he faced me with a softened expression. "Are you okay?"

I nodded, feeling the darts being launched from Maggie's stare.

Nikos turned back to Maggie and approached her. "You were leaving, weren't you?"

She chewed on her bottom lip. "Why do you have the key to her room?"

He ran his fingers through his hair and paced around her in a circle. "It's none of your business. How many times do I need to tell you to stop asking me personal questions?"

"What the hell are you doing here in her room?" She raised her voice. "Whenever I turn my back, you're screwing this bitch! Why? What's wrong with you?"

Nikos stopped to face her, his expression dark and somber. He crossed his arms over his chest.

"You need to get out, now. Don't you ever talk to Sabrina like this. I won't tolerate it."

She took a step back as if she were mulling over his words, scanned me from head to toe, and then threw herself at him, wrapping her arms around his neck. Nikos was as still as a statue. He kept his arms crossed over his chest and stared at her with a blank expression.

"Babe, let's get out of here and go to my room. I'll show you a good time, just like I used to. I'll make you so happy, Nikos."

She brought her face closer to his, attempting to kiss him. He tilted his head to avoid her lips, took her arms from around his neck, and held her by the wrists.

"Maggie, stop this circus right now. Stop pretending to be my girlfriend. Stop trying to control my life. Stop it. We have a business relationship, nothing more, and you know it. I'm seeing Sabrina now. Get over it."

She scoffed and freed her wrists from his grip with an abrupt gesture.

"You better think again, Nikos. I could make your life miserable if I decided to take my dad's sponsorship somewhere else. It's to your advantage to be with me. Without me, you can't do anything. Without me, you're nothing. You don't need this . . . this art teacher in your life. There's nothing she can do for you."

She eyed me with gritted teeth.

"If that's the case,"—he stepped toward the door and opened it—"you can leave now. You can't manipulate me, Maggie. If the condition for you to help the museum is to hold me hostage in a forced relationship, you can invest your money somewhere else. I've had enough." He waved at the open door, inviting Maggie to leave.

"You'll regret this, Nikos. You'll regret this decision. I swear you will."

Her eyes spewed poison at him before she stormed out of the room, ignoring me.

Nikos locked the door and came to me. I couldn't believe he'd finally told Maggie off in front of me. She was going to make our lives miserable, I was sure. His finger dabbed at my chin, and he lifted my head to face him. He smiled tenderly.

"Did she offend you because of me? How long was she here before I came in?"

I tried to return his smile, but I was still shaken. "Only a few minutes before you came in, but she was out of her mind."

"I won't permit her to offend you again. She's been getting on my nerves for too long, but she's gone too far now. Attacking you in your own room? I'm glad I came in. I hated to hear her insults. I hope she won't bother you again." He wrapped me in a protective embrace.

"Nikos, don't underestimate Maggie. She'll go to any lengths to get what she wants. And if she doesn't, she'll do what she can to damage us. As much as I hate this, I think you need to reconsider and find a way to work things out with her. You need her help for the museum."

I was afraid for Nikos. I was afraid Maggie was going to take drastic measures and stop sponsoring the museum and the exhibit. The financial instability of his country and the museum's finances were troubling him. And he was throwing away a tremendous opportunity because of me. I couldn't do anything to help him. All I was able to do was offer him my love and unconditional support.

He only held me tighter.

"She's not our only source of help. It'll take more effort on my part, and on the part of my associates, but we can get other sponsors and benefactors to raise funds for the museum. Don't worry about it. I'll figure something out."

I closed my eyes. I was secure in the arms of the man I loved and was happy he'd finally put an end to Maggie's advances in front of me. Yes, there was nothing going on between them, and now I was sure of it. And I trusted him more than ever.

"What do you want to do? Are you still up for dinner?"

I nodded. "Yes. I need to get dressed."

Instead of letting me go, Nikos's hands proceeded to the front of the bathrobe. He untied the knot, opening it to reveal my naked body. I trembled with excitement as I stared into his eyes, and when he touched me, the moisture between my legs revealed my burning desire.

"You're so beautiful, Sabrina. You have no idea how I have missed touching you." He caressed my nipples with his long, strong fingers.

I threw my arms around his broad shoulders. I had never wanted anyone as much as I wanted him. He was my dream. My god. My man. The kiss that followed was demanding and full of desire. His tongue invaded my mouth with an ardent craving. He left me breathless and absolutely at his mercy.

"And I love kissing you," he said, releasing me. "Now get dressed, goddess."

I gaped at him, frustrated. "Why do you always do this? You tease me and let me go. How can you? You know what you do to me."

"Self-control," he quipped.

As I frowned at him, he chuckled. "I love to see what I do to you."

Twelve

NIKOS DROVE US TO a small Italian restaurant not far from the hotel. Before we left, I prayed not to run into Maggie and was thankful we didn't see anyone. I'd told Curt I was going to dinner with Nikos, but he had no idea of what had happened in my room earlier. I doubted Maggie would tell him anything if she ran into him. It'd be humiliating for her to say she'd been in my room when Nikos came in. But anything was possible from Maggie, and that was what I feared. Once we'd sat down and ordered our meals, Nikos checked his cell phone.

"What happened?" I asked.

"There's something I don't quite understand." He shook his head. "I don't want to burden you with this, though."

"Nikos, please, tell me anything you want. I'm here for you. What is it you don't understand?"

He reached for my hand and squeezed it tight. "I'm intrigued. I'm not sure what to expect. It's about my brother's involvement in the Mycenaean jewels robbery. There's something missing in the story. I talked to him today. He's shaken, nervous, regretting the whole thing. He didn't think this would happen."

I nodded and waited for him to continue.

"He found out about the jewels when he heard my mother talking to me over the phone. He said he was hanging out with a group of petty thieves from Sicily and mentioned it to them in a conversation. Before he realized it, they had planned the heist and he was caught up in it. Well, a bunch of petty thieves from Sicily can't plan a robbery at this level. It was sophisticated, detailed."

The waiter brought two glasses of water and placed them on the table. Nikos took a sip before continuing. "They disappeared without a trace to Cyprus for several weeks. It doesn't make sense. Either Yannis is not telling the truth or he's been played. There were two other Sicilian men at the house where the Interpol agents found the jewels. No one's telling where the others are, but according to Yannis, there were five of them." He ran his fingers through his hair and frowned. "Something's not right."

"What are the agents saying? Didn't they find the same discrepancies?"

He shook his head. "I'm sure they're still investigating, but I won't get the scope of the case any longer. They found the jewels, so my participation and contribution to the case are over. As for Yannis, he'll be arraigned. He may be sentenced to prison for a few years, I imagine."

I had no words to comfort him. Nikos had acute gut instincts. Chances were he was right. He'd talked to his brother and he'd been to Cyprus. And Interpol had kept him informed of the details involving the heist from the beginning. They had recovered the jewels without the need to use the ransom money. Once the waiter brought our meals, Nikos changed the subject.

"We need to talk about our trip to Amphipolis. Tomorrow is your last day with the museum group. You are taking a trip to Delphi, right?"

"Yes, it's our last stop. We've been having a great time."

"I've made arrangements for you to keep your room at the hotel here in Athens for another week. That way you don't have to pack all your things to come to Amphipolis. We should be there for a few days. I rescheduled your flight for the following Saturday. When we come back from Amphipolis, you'll still have some time in Athens. I'll bring you with me to the museum if you want."

"I can't believe you've planned it all out. How did you have time for all this?"

"I have a fabulous assistant. You'll meet Athena when we go to Amphipolis. She's the best archaeologist on my team, and she's looking forward to meeting you. She's been invaluable in helping the team during my absence. And she takes care of administrative issues for me as well. She's made the arrangements for our trip."

Oh. Another woman. And I hadn't even heard of this one before. Athena. Did I have any reason to be ridiculously apprehensive knowing there was a woman on his team who did everything for him? *Get the stupid thoughts out of your head before he reads your mind, Sabrina! You don't even know anything about her. Stop being so jealous of Nikos! He wants you, doesn't he? He told Maggie off in front of you, didn't he? What other proof do you need he's into you?* Argh! Why did I have to be so insecure about Nikos? I forced a smile before he sensed my anxiety.

"Awesome! I can't wait to meet the other members of your team. I'm so excited about this trip." I took a sip of my water.

"I'm sure you'll love it. Athena will keep you company whenever I'm busy."

The waiter brought us cappuccinos and handed Nikos the bill.

"Are you ready to go back to the hotel?" he asked once he'd finished his cup.

I shook my head. He raised his eyebrows.

"Not to the hotel." I smiled. "I want to spend the night with you somewhere else."

"What do you have in mind? It's too late to go to Cape Sounion."

He smiled his absurd and rakish grin, making me blush.

"I wish." I giggled, remembering the eyes of the gods upon us while we shone inside the Temple of Poseidon. I put on a straight face, leaned forward over the table with my hand under my chin, and looked deeply into his eyes.

"I want to go to your place."

He leaned back in his chair. His smile turned into a frown, and his jaw tightened. He rubbed his chin, staring at me without blinking.

"My place?"

I nodded. What was the problem with taking me to his home? He looked uncomfortable. *Nikos, I need you to trust me. Take me to your home. Let me get to know you. Tell me what has made you afraid of showing your emotions.*

"I've been here for about a week, and you haven't taken me to your house yet. I don't want to go back to the hotel tonight. Not after that altercation with Maggie, not knowing she may be lurking around. I want to be with you and not worry about her."

He continued to rub his chin, studying me. Did I overstep my boundaries? Was it too early to ask to go to his home? No. I had to know where he lived, how he lived. He'd been to my apartment. I wanted to go to his. I had to know more about him in his own environment. He closed his eyes and inhaled deeply. When he opened them again, his smile returned and he seemed to have already composed himself after the shock of my request.

"We'll go, then."

His answer took me by surprise, although it's what I wanted to hear. My heart pounded like a hammer, and I looked at him wide-eyed with excitement. I was going to his place. Would he finally open up to me?

We drove through a part of town I hadn't seen yet, but it didn't take long for us to arrive. He parked the car in a well-lit street and led me to a quaint stucco three-story building. We climbed the steps to the second floor, and he unlocked the door. There was only one apartment per floor. As he stepped inside and turned the light on, he waved for me to enter.

"Welcome, my goddess."

I walked in with caution, afraid to desecrate the holiness of his sanctuary. The living room was large and looked like a museum. What else would I have expected? There were bits and pieces of archaeological artifacts scattered around. Some of them were labeled as if they were prepared for an exhibition. Frames filled with pictures of his excavations and archaeological accomplishments hung on the walls, along with newspaper clips featuring him in different capacities: Nikos receiving prizes, shaking hands with dignitaries, digging, and even teaching. A huge, comfortable-looking brown leather couch stood at one side of the large room with a side table next to it. On top of the table, a single picture frame stood as the only decoration. On the other side of the room, opposite from the couch, stood an antique desk with a computer, which might have been his workstation.

"I don't spend a lot of time at home." He stood by the door, watching me. "I wasn't expecting to bring anyone here. I just work and sleep here. This is my office."

It was easy to realize he was, indeed, totally committed to his job, to his work. It was his passion, his life, as his mother had said. His dedication was visible even in his home. His work surrounded him.

"It's perfect for you." I looked around the room, admiring some of the objects and the photos and frames hanging on the walls. I walked past the side table and noticed the beautiful frame on it. It displayed a photo of him with another woman. She was beautiful, with long brown hair and huge, heavy-lidded eyes. She was hugging him from behind, her arms encircling his neck. His face was carefree and serene, exhibiting a radiant smile I hadn't seen before. My breath caught in my throat. Who was this woman he seemed to be so happy with? I picked up the frame and studied their faces. Who was the woman he seemed to be so *in love* with seemed to be the more appropriate question. I chewed on my bottom lip.

Nikos cleared his throat. "Would you care for something to drink?"

"Who is she?" I pointed to the pretty face in the picture. My jealousy had ascended to a level beyond what I thought possible. Not even Maggie had elicited such an irrational response from me. I couldn't help myself.

"She's gone." His tone was dry and impassive.

"Gone where? Who is she?" The picture frame was shaking in my hands.

"It doesn't matter now, Sabrina. She's . . . she's gone," he repeated.

"Why don't you want to tell me anything about you and your life?" My voice didn't come out loud enough. I knew I was being unreasonable, but all the doubts and insecurity I had over him were back, and in full force.

He came toward me, took the frame away, and set it back on the table with the photo facing the wall, before taking me into his arms. His smoky, dark eyes made me melt as his hands slid underneath my blouse and his fingers ran down my back, causing goosebumps on my skin.

"Why are you so jealous? I told you she's gone. Don't think about my past. I'm here with you right now, am I not?" His fingers caressed my skin under the blouse while he hypnotized me.

"I want to get to know you, Nikos." I sighed. "What made you build a wall around your heart? Was it because of her?"

He stared at me with intensity while his fingers tickled my back.

"I don't want to talk about it now. I don't want to talk about my past. Don't bring anyone else into our moment. Don't concern yourself with anyone else in my life, past or present. You're the only I want to be with, Sabrina. Don't you trust me?"

I put my arms around his neck. The thought of him with someone else hurt like a knife piercing through me. "You looked so happy with her."

He lowered his head and brushed his lips against mine, making my whole body tingle.

"I'm happy with you." He pulled me closer to him, and his hard length pressed against me. His lips found mine again, and his tongue invaded my mouth in a breathless and ardent kiss. I was still panting when he released me.

"Then let me in," I begged. "Please. Let me in."

"I never bring anyone to my place. You're the first one in a long time. You're in more than you can realize." He grabbed the hem of my shirt and lifted it over my head, removing my bra and baring my upper body. His strong, masculine hands cupped my breasts, stroking my nipples with his thumbs. My heart beat fast, and I gave a loud sigh.

"Do you know what you do to me?" I whispered.

"I do. And I love your reactions whenever I touch you. I want you, Sabrina."

He picked me up and carried me to a dark room, placing me gently on a bed. A soft glow illuminated the room when he turned on a lamp, and I realized I was in his bedroom. It looked quite the opposite of the other room. It wasn't filled with antique furniture and decorations resembling an archaeological museum. Instead, it combined black and white with effortless style, resulting in a very modern design.

The white walls were bare except for a huge black-and-white painting that resembled a Rothko. Under the painting, there was a modern wingback chair. Contemporary glass column lamps decorated the bed tables flanking the king size bed, while the white sheets and classic comforter contrasted with the black upholstered headboard. Soft white pillows completed the fashionable look. The simple yet exquisite decoration gave the room a fresh, stunning effect.

While checking out his trendy bedroom, I almost missed when he took his shirt off and tossed it on the floor. Admiring his chiseled body was enough for the sexual tension to build within me even more. Nikos exuded sensuality, and I longed to touch him and squirm beneath his body. He unzipped his jeans and slid them off his muscular legs, revealing how hard he was. I bit my lower lip, and my pulse quickened. I couldn't get enough of him. My attraction to him overwhelmed my senses.

He climbed into bed next to where he'd laid me and leaned over to remove my skirt and underwear, all the while looking at me with desire before turning me around to start massaging my shoulders.

"You don't need to be jealous," he whispered in my ear. "You're the only woman I want. I'll show you."

His long fingers rubbed my tense muscles with a steady, circular motion. A soft moan escaped my lips when his warm tongue trailed down my neck. He licked me with firm, wet strokes, as if I were the most delicious dessert he'd ever tasted.

As his fingers glided down to massage my buttocks, he kissed the curve of my lower back, making my skin quiver with pleasure. I squirmed beneath his hands and mouth, savoring his worship of my body. As he lifted my hips and my knees curled under my body, his tongue and lips slid to the inside of my thighs. I clutched at the sheets when he inserted his finger inside of me. He worked his tongue back and forth, licking and kissing each inch of my sensitive skin with passionate intensity. My hips danced in anticipation of the coming orgasm. When I reached my climax, I buried my head in the pillows, muffling the scream that exploded from me while I shuddered with indescribable pleasure. Wave after wave of sexual rapture washed over me. I was close to being breathless when he penetrated me. My inner muscles took his thick length all the way, contracting in quick spasms.

His hands held onto my hips as he allowed my body to grow accustomed to his rhythm. I gasped and shuddered as his possessive thrusts filled me with a throbbing heat. I tightened my inner hold on him until he reached his climax with a stifled growl. Nikos released me and rolled me over. The smirk on his face intensified when his hungry eyes met mine. I threw my arms around his neck and pulled his head down to mine. His lips touched mine with a light stroke before his tongue invaded my mouth to kiss me hungrily. His hands caressed my swollen breasts, and he pinched my nipples, making me arch as an intense pleasure pulsated through my groin.

"Oh, Nikos," I moaned in between his kisses. "I want you. I love to feel you inside of me."

He climbed on me as if my words had been a command. Without taking his mouth from mine, he penetrated me again with a wild urgency. His hands lifted mine above my head to hold me captive. I wrapped my legs around his waist, feeling him slide in and out of me, pushing deeper and harder. His mouth left mine, and he buried his head against my neck until he let out a satiated moan. He rolled to the side and lay by me; sweat dripped from his forehead. He touched my face with the back of his hand.

"Sabrina," he mumbled.

"What?" I brushed my lips on his ears.

He shook his head and gave a deep sigh. Whatever he had been about to tell me seemed to get locked inside his mind. Instead of saying anything else, he planted a kiss on my lips and hugged me tight. I rested my head on his shoulder.

"What time is the bus leaving for Delphi in the morning?" he asked.

"Nine."

"Good. I'll drop you at the hotel by eight, then."

He kissed me again. "I have the whole night to show you how much I want you."

Thirteen

A FAINT LIGHT ILLUMINATED the room, and I rubbed my eyes, becoming aware I was in Nikos's bed.

"Good morning, beautiful." I heard his husky voice and saw him standing by the bed, holding a breakfast tray. He hadn't bothered to dress, and his naked body radiated sexiness from every pore. I stared in disbelief when I realized he was as hard as he'd been all night long.

Pulling myself up into a sitting position, I received the tray he handed me. Nikos was bringing me breakfast in bed! He lowered his head to give me a soft kiss on the lips.

"How are you feeling?"

I cleared my throat. "Fabulous. I feel like a goddess."

His lustful smile shone. I was exhausted but satiated and feeling like the luckiest woman on the planet, waking up in the bed of the man I loved. We'd made love all night, and he'd cooked me breakfast. I was his goddess. The only thing missing was for him to finally open up to me and trust me enough to tell me all about his life. I wanted him to tell me who the woman in the picture was. I wanted him to tell me what had happened in his past. I wanted him to tell me he loved me. She might be the person he'd loved long ago as his mother had hinted. I had to be strong and patient. After all, he'd brought me to his place and shown me how much he wanted me. This I could tell. But I wanted more. I wanted his love.

"I hope you enjoy it," he said. "I'll take a shower to cool off and get ready. Seeing you in bed eating breakfast is making me hungry for you again."

He gave me a long, seductive stare that made me blush before he walked away to the bathroom. I turned my attention back to the tray to look at my sumptuous breakfast. A glass of orange juice, a cup of cappuccino, scrambled eggs, a croissant, and a bowl of strawberries. Nikos had outdone himself again. I couldn't believe he'd cooked breakfast for me. After I finished eating, I placed the tray on the bedside table. Nikos came out of the bathroom with a towel wrapped around his waist.

"Your turn, goddess," he said, pointing to the bathroom.

I got out of bed and picked up the tray. "Show me where the kitchen is so I can clean this up."

He shook his head. "Leave it there. You're my guest."

"I should at least put it back in the kitchen," I insisted.

He opened the closet, looking for something to wear. "As you please, princess. The kitchen is right next to the living room, to the left."

I stepped out of the bedroom and walked past the living room to find a small clean kitchen. I set the tray on the counter, and on my way back to the bedroom, I instinctively searched for the picture and picked it up again, studying the happy faces of Nikos and the pretty young woman. I was so engrossed in my thoughts, trying to figure out what she'd possibly meant to him, that I didn't realize Nikos stood next to me. With a gasp, I jumped back in surprise as he gently took the frame from me and put it back on the table with the picture still facing the wall. He stepped closer and cupped my face.

"If it bothers you so much, why do you keep looking at it?" His eyes emanated a sadness I couldn't quite understand.

"I don't know." I swallowed a gulp of air. "You look so happy in the picture, so in love."

He brought my face closer to his.

"It was a long time ago, Sabrina," he whispered. "Whatever happened is in the past; it doesn't matter now." He kissed me with a renewed intensity. I immersed myself in the power of his kiss. I had to drop the doubts, the insecurity. The woman in the picture had been special to him for sure. Otherwise, her picture wouldn't have a prominent place in his living room. But she no longer belonged in his life. I wanted to believe him. I had to believe him. I had to stop pressuring him to tell me about his past. I had to be patient, as his mother had asked me to. I had to be confident that he'd tell me about it when he was ready to open up to me. I knew I'd made progress. At least he'd told Maggie to get out of his life, and he'd brought me to his home—all of these in less than twenty-four hours. Nikos was all I ever wanted, and he was letting me in little by little. What else could I wish for?

"Go get ready, my beautiful, or you'll miss Delphi," he said as he released me from his passionate kiss. His eyes scanned my naked body from head to toe. "I'm trying hard not to throw you in bed and taste you again."

Blushing under his gaze, I skipped to the bathroom to take a shower.

When he parked the car in front of the hotel, I hesitated before getting out. The image of an angry Maggie flashed in my mind. I didn't want to cross paths with her anymore while in Greece. Nikos seemed to be aware of my hesitation.

"Don't worry. Go have fun and enjoy your last day with the group." He touched my hair softly and hooked a loose strand behind my ear.

I rested my head on his shoulder. "Will I see you tonight?"

"What are your plans?" He continued playing with the strand of my hair.

"There's a farewell dinner for the group, and I need to attend," I said. "It's the last night."

"Then enjoy it with your friends. Tell Curt I wish him a good trip back home to Houston. I'll see you in the morning. Our flight to Amphipolis is at 11 a.m. I'll be here at 9, which should give us plenty of time. You don't need to check out of your room; just pack light."

I sighed. "I miss you already."

He lifted my chin and kissed me. The touch of his lips didn't fail to ignite the passion within me.

"I'll be dreaming about you when I put my head on my pillow. Your perfume is all over my bed now." He breathed against my neck. "Have fun and don't worry about anything. Enjoy Delphi and the get-together. I'll see you in the morning, and if you need me, call me."

I entered the hotel with apprehension but was immediately greeted by Curt. He stood in the lobby with a worried expression.

"Baby girl, are you okay? I was worried sick about you." He hugged me tightly. "Thank the gods of Olympus you're here."

"I'm fine, Curt. I need to go to my room and change before we get on the bus to Delphi."

I rushed him to the elevator. I didn't want to be in the lobby in case Maggie showed up.

"You were with Nikos, right?" he asked when we entered my room.

"You guessed right. He just dropped me off."

"Yes, of course. I ran into Medusa last night. And she's spitting fire through her nostrils. For real. She said she hates both of you. She didn't get into details, but she was furious she has to stay in Athens for another couple of days."

"What did she tell you?" I picked out a pair of jeans and a T-shirt and went into the bathroom to change.

"Her father's friend who paid a fortune to borrow the jewels is coming from London. He arrives tomorrow morning. They were going to fly the jewels to him, but he's decided to take them in person. So instead of going to London, Maggie has to wait for him here in Athens. What happened between you two?"

I came out of the bathroom and sat on the bed. Curt stood in front of the balcony, looking out at the Acropolis.

"In a nutshell, Nikos told her to leave him alone. In front of me."

Curt faced me, his eyes popping out of his head. His mouth dropped open. "What?"

"She came in here last night to confront me about him. Nikos walked in on us. She was beside herself when she realized he had a key to the room. He told her she had to stop pretending to be his girlfriend."

Curt stared at me wide-eyed and didn't say a word. He motioned for me to continue.

"She threatened to take her sponsorship to another museum if he didn't choose her. But he opened the door and told her to go because he'd made up his mind and he was seeing me."

Curt came toward the bed and sat next to me. "Blessed Oracle of Delphi! How did I miss that? What I wouldn't give to have been there." He laughed out loud. "Gods of Olympus help us. Pandora's box has been opened."

I sighed. "Yeah. To tell you the truth, Curt, I'm so worried for Nikos. He doesn't seem fazed at all. But if she takes her sponsorship somewhere else, his museum will be in worse trouble. I even asked him to reconsider."

"Are you out of your mind? Asking him to reconsider being with her? I don't think so. It was high time he told her off. She's been on his nerves for a long time. I've always wondered how long he'd put up with her crap."

"But it's his job, Curt. And it can't be easy to get an organization such as Mr. Wallendorf's to subsidize museum exhibitions."

"Yes, that will be tough. But I'm sure Nikos can find an alternative." He shook his head. "We need to hope for the best. In the meantime, she's still around and I'm worried about you."

"I'm staying in Greece for another week with Nikos. Tomorrow morning, we're taking a plane to Kavala, and from there we're renting a car to Amphipolis to see the new excavation site. We'll be there for a few days. By the time I get back to Athens, I'm sure she'll be in London with her father's British art-collector friend. I can't wait!"

"I can't believe how lucky you are. Another week in Greece with our god. Nikos has been such a great influence!"

I nodded. "I'll miss you, Curt. This week has been fantastic. Thank you so much for being such a wonderful friend." I threw my arms around him in a friendly embrace.

"Don't make me cry; we still have a beautiful day ahead of us. By the way, I won't forgive you for leaving me by myself to tell Jane and Robert about our trip. Jane will torture me to find out all about it."

We took the elevator to the lobby to meet Dr. Gould, who was already there with most of the guests. The bus waited for us in front of the hotel, and we were ready to take our day trip.

Delphi was one of the most famous archaeological sites in Greece. It was located on the slope of Mount Parnassus, overlooking the Pleistos Valley. The drive was scenic and beautiful, and along the way we passed by the agricultural center of Beotia and the birthplace of King Oedipus, the city of Theva.

We had a wonderful time visiting the sanctuary of Apollo, the site of the ancient Oracle, and telling our guests beautiful stories from ancient Greek history and mythology. The ancient Greeks thought Delphi was the middle of the earth. The Greeks consulted the Oracle before all major undertakings, especially wars and the founding of colonies, as she exerted considerable influence throughout the Greek world. The the site was as magical as all the other archaeological places I'd visited in Greece. I was proud of myself for feeling so comfortable in my knowledge, as if I'd been there before—as if I'd lived in Greece. Speaking Greek was the only thing I lacked to feel I belonged there fully. I wished Nikos had been there with me. Maybe I'd come back to Delphi with him someday.

After a three-hour exploration of the site, we drove back. The bus passed through the picturesque mountain village of Arachova, built on the southern slopes of Mount Parnassus, where we stopped for last-minute souvenirs. The town was well known for its hand-woven carpets, rugs, and quilts and delicious wine and cheese. I was already feeling nostalgic, missing a place I'd been in for barely a week. Curt bought a handful of souvenirs, glad we'd had this last-minute stop.

Back in Athens, we had no time to rest before meeting with the group again for our farewell dinner. I walked in and out of the hotel in full awareness. I wanted to make sure Maggie's presence wouldn't surprise me or spoil the rest of my evening.

Dr. Gould chose a typical Greek tavern in the historical Pláka neighborhood. It served classic Greek dishes, and we watched an exuberant performance of traditional dancing, music, and plate-smashing. We had a lot of fun, and by the time we got back to the hotel, I was tired but elated to have had such a great experience.

Curt accompanied me to my room to say goodbye. His flight to Houston wouldn't leave until after lunch, but my flight to Amphipolis was earlier so I wasn't going to see him again for a week.

"This has been the most memorable time of my life," he said.

"Without a doubt," I agreed. "I'll miss you, Curt. It will only be for a week, but I miss you already."

He chuckled. "I'll miss you, too, my love. Now, listen. If you ever see Medusa again, be cool. Pretend she's not there. Don't engage in any conversation with her. But I hope you won't see her again. When you get back to Houston, we'll devise a plan on how to deal with her."

I hugged him and gave him a quick kiss on his cheek.

"I love you, Curt. Have a great trip tomorrow, and tell Jane and Robert I miss them. I'm sure Jane isn't happy with me since I haven't been keeping in touch."

"She'll have to wait for you. I won't say a word."

We laughed until we hurt. We knew Jane wouldn't leave Curt alone until she heard enough of our adventures in Greece.

Fourteen

AFTER SAYING GOODBYE TO Curt, I packed for the flight, took a hot shower, and tried to sleep. But I was too excited to relax, and by seven I had ordered room service to avoid a chance encounter with Maggie. I wondered if Nikos was aware she hadn't left Athens yet.

At nine, he entered the room looking as provocative as ever in a pair of light jeans and a dark green polo that complemented his luscious tanned skin. His strong arms encircled my waist.

"How is my goddess doing today?" His lips brushed mine.

"Much better, now that you're here with me." I returned his quick kiss.

"Did you have a good time yesterday?"

"Yes. Delphi was wonderful! I'd love to go there again with you someday. It was a great trip."

"I'll take you there sometime." He pulled me closer and kissed me again. His arousal bulged against the front of his jeans and I wanted to feel him inside of me, but there was no time. He released me and paced around the room, running his fingers through his hair.

"What's bothering you?" I asked.

"A slight change of plans." He sat on the bed.

I raised my eyebrows and waited for him to continue.

"I can't leave Athens today, but I'm taking you to the airport.

Athena will wait for you in Kavala, and she'll drive you to Amphipolis. She'll take care of you until I get there."

I gaped at him, at a loss for words. I couldn't believe what he was saying. This was not just a slight change of plans; it was a total change of plans. He stood up and came close to me, cupping my head with his hands.

"You'll be fine. I want you to stay with Athena the whole time."

"What happened? Why can't you go with me?" My voice broke.

Nikos sighed. "Mr. Green's in town, and he's requested my presence. The museum director asked me to delay the trip for a day or two so I can take care of him."

I looked at him, surprised. "Who is Mr. Green?"

"He's Mr. Wallendorf's friend, the British art collector who's borrowing the Mycenaean jewels. He wasn't supposed to be in Athens. The jewels were being taken to him in London, but he decided to come for the transfer in person." He held me by the waist, pressing me close to him.

I knew this was true. And I knew Maggie would be there too. I shook my head. "Curt bumped into Maggie in the hotel, and she told him about it. She wasn't happy to stay in Athens for another couple of days."

"Unfortunately, I'll have to go to dinner with both of them. I'm not sure how I'll deal with Maggie, but at this point I'll play along to not upset anyone. This has escalated all out of proportion. I can't wait to get it over with."

I put my arms around his neck. "When are you coming to meet me in Amphipolis, then?"

"I've changed my flight to tomorrow evening. I'll rent a car to drive to Amphipolis, and we'll spend the night together." His fingers caressed my back.

"Why don't I stay here and go with you tomorrow, then?"

"No. You don't need to waste your time in Athens by yourself while I'm busy with Maggie and Mr. Green. I'd feel much better if you're in Amphipolis with Athena. I thought about bringing you to my place, but visiting the site will be a much better experience for you."

His sharp, piercing eyes met mine with determination. He wasn't about to let me stay in Athens.

"Are you ready to go to the airport?" He released me and ran his fingers through his hair again before picking up my duffle bag. It was a bad time for me to be in Athens. I regretted having asked him to visit Amphipolis. The last thing he needed was to worry about me.

During the ride to the airport, he talked about Amphipolis and the latest discoveries. And he instructed me again to stay close to Athena. "Have a safe trip. I'll be with you tomorrow. Call me when you get settled. Athena will keep you company."

He hugged me tightly, and I inhaled his musky scent.

"I'm sorry I'm causing you so much trouble, Nikos. I don't want to bother Athena, either. If she has work to do, I have no problem being by myself."

"No, you're not causing any trouble. And you won't bother Athena, either. I don't want you wandering on your own. Promise me you'll stay with her at the excavation site."

His frown and serious tone worried me.

"Okay, then. I'll stay with Athena. I promise."

I had no idea why it was so important that I promise to stay with Athena. But I didn't want to argue, so it was better to agree with him. His mouth brushed against mine, and he bit my lower lip just enough to arouse me. I wrapped my arms around his shoulders and brought him closer, deepening the kiss. Another night without him. It was hard to believe my days in Athens had been so tumultuous.

"You're going to miss the plane if you keep kissing me like this." He smacked his lips while his dark eyes appeared to strip me naked. "I'll make up for it when I see you tomorrow. Now, you better go, my goddess."

The hour flight from Athens to Kavala was on time, and soon I was disembarking at the small airport. A beautiful, olive-skinned woman wearing jeans and a white blouse stood at the baggage claim area holding a sign with my name on it. Her hair was black, long, and curly, and she wore gold round-framed glasses. Athena was beautiful. I approached her with caution.

"Sabrina?" she asked as I walked toward her.

"Yes. Athena?"

She nodded and extended a hand with a friendly smile.

"I'm delighted to meet you," she said with a heavy accent.

I shook her hand. "Me too. Nikos has said wonderful things about you. Thank you so much for coming to Kavala to pick me up. I'm sorry I have to bother you with this, but Nikos insisted I come without him."

"Yes. The issue with the Mycenaean jewels has taken its toll on all of us. Nikos is not happy to be in Athens right now, but he'll be here tomorrow and we can close this chapter once and for all."

I followed her to the car parked outside the airport. During the hour drive, she told me about the site, what they were doing, and how the work was progressing. It sounded fascinating, and I was glad I'd be able to visit it.

Soon, she parked in front of a pink two-story building, and we walked in. Pension Delfini was a small beachfront hotel on the outskirts of Amphipolis. It had only eleven rooms, and they all had balconies facing the Aegean Sea. Athena talked to the front desk attendant, who handed me a room key.

"This is a small hotel, but it has a beautiful view. It's the closest place to the site that had an available room. I hope you don't mind sharing the room with Nikos."

She was smirking. I wasn't sure if she was being sarcastic or jealous or if she simply wanted proof I was sleeping with Nikos. I chose to ignore it.

"Thanks for arranging the room on such short notice."

"You're welcome. Do you need to refresh yourself? I want to get to the site as soon as possible."

"I'll drop my things in the room and will be right back. Would you like to come up with me?"

"I'll wait for you here in the lobby."

I climbed the steps to the second floor, where my room was. I wanted to explore the place by myself. I wasn't in the mood to be with Athena the whole day. I hadn't quite figured her out, and I hadn't sorted out my feelings for her either, although deep down I was jealous to learn she worked with Nikos. She was beautiful and intelligent, and he hadn't stopped complimenting her. Maybe once I was at the site, she'd get busy and leave me alone for a while.

The room was simple, clean, and small, with a queen-size bed taking up most of the space. Bedside tables stood on either side of the bed, and a flower-printed curtain opened onto the balcony. A small kitchenette with a refrigerator completed the setup. It was a nice touch. I left my duffle bag on the bed, washed my face and hands, and went back downstairs. Athena offered me a bottle of water.

"Okay, let's go to the site. I'm sure you'll enjoy it."

We arrived on an unpaved road that arched toward a steep cliff. Athena parked the car, and we approached the entrance, where scaffolds were mounted. Men and women excavated and cleaned recently uncovered artifacts. Nikos's team of archaeologists had found an almost-intact skeleton inside a tomb from the time of Alexander the Great. They were ready to make a formal announcement, and since Nikos was the chief archaeologist, they expected him to release the statement. The burial site was the largest ever discovered in Greece, and they had plenty of reason to be proud about it.

"Please be careful as you walk about," Athena cautioned as we approached the burial site. "The tomb dates from the late fourth century BC. Amphipolis was a major city of the Macedonian Kingdom at that time. It's a wonderful find, and I can't wait for Nikos to see it in person."

"This is amazing. I'd love to work on an excavation site like this. Have you found out who the skeleton might have been?" I followed Athena.

"Not yet. All we've discovered at this point is it's a male who was most likely a general. There are still many areas we need to explore. We found a carved stone lion, two sphinxes, two caryatids, and a large floor mosaic in the earlier stages of the excavation. You're knowledgeable about Greek ancient history, right?"

I nodded. "It's what I'm studying. I've always loved Greek history."

"I'm sure you have. We all love it. That's why we're on Nikos's team." She paused, looked at me for a brief moment, and sighed. "You're so lucky."

"Lucky? Why do you say that?" I wasn't sure what she meant, but her tone and the way she'd paused to look back at me made me uncomfortable.

"What I mean is that Nikos is . . . how can I say it . . . well, he's too involved in his work. He's never interested in dating anyone." Athena cleared her throat. "Not even the people who are closer to him and have so much in common with him . . . until he met you."

I raised my eyebrows. "Why are you saying this?"

A faint grin showed on her face, and she put her hands in her pockets. "Sabrina, please don't get me wrong. All the women around here are crazy about Nikos and wish he'd go out with them. But he refuses to get involved with anyone in his field, be it a student, a teacher, or an archaeologist. In fact, I've never seen him interested in anyone like he's into you, believe me."

My lips twitched when I heard her say all the women she knew were crazy about Nikos and wanted him. If she'd intended to make me jealous, she'd accomplished it. I didn't want to reveal much about my relationship with Nikos to her, but I had no idea how much he'd told her about me. The blood rushed to my face.

"We were wondering how you were able to penetrate his fortress," she continued.

I shook my head. "I haven't penetrated his fortress. I don't know what you're talking about."

"Don't be silly. He's head over heels in love with you; can't you tell?" She turned around and signaled for me to follow her.

Why did she assume Nikos was in love with me? Did he tell her? I followed her to the entrance of the tomb, where the two sphinxes stood guard. The stone sculptures were well preserved and several archaeologists worked around them. Athena approached a tall, good-looking dark-haired man. He was wearing cargo shorts and a light-brown button-down shirt that highlighted his athletic physique. His tanned skin was proof he worked outdoors. A teenage boy stood next to him holding a wooden-handled trowel and a brush.

"Herete, Aleksy; herete, Theo." She hugged the boy and gave him a kiss on the cheek before saying something to them in Greek. Then she turned to me. "This is Sabrina, Nikos's guest. She's a student from Houston. Aleksy is one of our main archaeologists working on the site. Theo is Nikos's sponsored student, but he doesn't speak much English."

A guest and a student from Houston, she'd said. I wondered if Nikos had told her to introduce me as his student. The label kept following me. The friendly-looking teenager bowed to me, showing respect. It reminded me of Nikos's demeanor. Aleksy looked me over from head to toe, making me shudder, before he extended his hand to greet me.

"It's a pleasure to meet you. I can show you around." He held my hand a little longer than usual.

"Thank you." I pulled my hand from his tight grip. "Did you excavate most of the tomb? I'd love to hear about it."

"I've been digging most of it, yes," he said, winking at me. "What about dinner tonight? I'll pick you up and show you a great time. You're staying at Pension Delfini, right?"

"Yes, I'm staying at Pension Delfini. I'm sure you have lots of great stories about your archaeology digs, but Nikos—"

"She's busy tonight, Aleksy," Athena interfered. "Maybe another time."

"What about Nikos?" Aleksy looked at me with curiosity, ignoring Athena. "Wasn't he supposed to be here today?"

"Nikos got delayed," I said. "He's still tied up in the Mycenaean jewels mess, but he'll be here tomorrow."

Aleksy winked at me again. "Too bad. I'll hook up with you later and show you around."

"Don't bother, Aleksy," Athena insisted. "I'll show Sabrina around. Take good care of Theo. Nikos wants a report on his progress." Athena gave Theo another kiss on the cheek. The boy lowered his gaze, obviously embarrassed.

Aleksy rolled his eyes. "Sure."

I followed Athena to the other side of the tomb. "Why does Nikos want a report on Theo? Who is he?" I asked when we were out of earshot.

"Theo's one of Nikos's sponsored students. Hasn't he told you?"

I shook my head. "No, he hasn't."

"Well, Nikos has a small nonprofit. It helps underprivileged high school kids stay in school and take an interest in Greek history. Nikos helps them study archaeology and art history in college to be successful students. And become future historians or archaeologists."

"I had no idea about this." One more thing Nikos hadn't told me about his life. I realized more and more that I knew so little about the man I was so in love with.

"Nikos is trying to raise awareness about our rich culture and history. He does a great job. He spends a lot of time with these students on the weekends. He teaches them, mentors them, makes sure they're ready for the future. He donates most of his salary to this effort, and we all pitch in. We love to have his students come out to the field."

Her words were so full of pride it was obvious Athena loved him, and it made me uneasy. I wondered if they had ever been more than coworkers. I had to control my jealousy. We strolled along the area while she showed me some of the excavations. A man carrying a clipboard approached her and asked something in Greek. She introduced me to him before excusing herself. They needed to discuss the logistics about one of their most recent findings.

I sat on the steps of the tomb while they talked and took a sip of water. I wanted to explore the place by myself, find the floor mosaic depicting a man with a laurel wreath driving a chariot drawn by horses and led by the god Hermes. All I wanted was to absorb this beautiful place on my own. And I wanted to sort out my feelings. I'd learned more about Nikos, and I had to make sense of his life. Without waiting for Athena, I got up and walked toward the tomb's entrance. I was hoping to go inside and take a peek at the mosaic.

"Where are you going?" Athena soon caught up to me, startling me.

I sighed. "Athena, thank you for keeping me company; I appreciate it. But I can see you're busy and you don't need to babysit me the whole time I'm here. I can take a look on my own. I don't mind; I mean it."

She shook her head. "No, you can't."

I stared at her, raising my arms. "What do you mean, I can't? What's the problem? I'm a grown woman, and it's not as if I'm going to destroy the site or remove something from it."

"Nikos instructed me not to leave you." Her voice was resolute.

"And do you have to do whatever he tells you?"

Athena gritted her teeth. "After what happened in Santorini, Sabrina, I'm shocked he even allowed you to come to the site. Why can't you understand that?"

I tilted my head and gaped at her. "What happened in Santorini? What are you talking about?"

"Oh, my big mouth. He hasn't told you about that either, has he? Of course he hasn't. I shouldn't have mentioned it. Sorry." Athena removed her glasses, looked down at the ground, and scratched her head. She seemed lost in her thoughts and upset with herself. She kicked some loosened rocks on the ground and avoided looking at me. I grabbed her arms and forced her to look at me. I needed answers.

"Athena, tell me what happened in Santorini. Look at me, please. I feel like a stupid child that can't be left alone for one minute. You told me Nikos was in love with me, but how do you know? Help me to understand Nikos. Help me to understand what happened to him."

She looked at me briefly before staring down at the ground again. "Sabrina, I can't. I can't tell you anything. I can't tell you about Nikos's life. I'm sorry."

"Athena, please. Please. I beg you, please tell me. I need to understand him. Please tell me what happened in Santorini." I shook her arms lightly.

"I can't, Sabrina. I'm not going to betray Nikos's trust. I'm hating myself right now for saying so much already. Nikos will be beyond disappointed when he finds out I can't control my big mouth. If he hasn't told you about it, then you'll have to wait 'til he feels it's the right time to do so."

Tears flooded my eyes, and I bit my lips, forcing back the tears. I didn't want to cry in front of Athena. I let go of her and turned away.

"Sabrina." She came after me. "I understand your frustration. Nikos has always been a distant person . . . he's so private and lonely. You've no idea how lucky you are that he's allowed you so far into his life."

I didn't want to argue with her or beg her to tell me about Nikos anymore. Athena seemed to know a lot about Nikos, and I didn't like it.

"No, you can't understand my frustration, Athena. I live miles away from Nikos. I can't see him every day. I have no time to get to know him better. I have a week 'til I get back to Houston. And you know what? Maybe it's not worth it. For sure, he's a private person, and he doesn't feel comfortable sharing his past with me. I don't see how he's in love with me when he doesn't allow me into his life, when he doesn't tell me his secrets."

Athena came around to confront me, red in the face. "What are you talking about? Are you the only one who can't tell he's in love with you? I've been friends with Nikos for years, and this is the first time I've seen him like this. He's so protective of you. He plans his moves wondering if you'll be happy about it. His voice changes when he mentions your name. I wish he was like this with me!"

"With you?" I gasped. I wasn't expecting her to confirm what I'd been suspecting.

"Yes, but he's not. It's you who's captured his heart. He hurts, too, Sabrina, and I'm sure he's doing all he can to protect you from his wounds. He's not hiding his past from you on purpose. He just doesn't know how to forget."

I shook my head and took a deep breath. Athena continued.

"This doesn't solve anything, but trust me. Be patient with Nikos. He's worth it; oh, he's so worth it! How could you even think about giving up on him?" Her voice was shaky.

Yes, she was in love with him. How could I have doubted it? Athena stepped away from the tomb's main entrance. I followed her.

"Athena, please wait."

When she stopped to face me, tears were trickling down her face. How did this argument become her issue? She rubbed away her tears with the back of her hands.

"I'm sorry, Sabrina. I don't want to see Nikos suffer. He's the best boss, the best teacher, the best friend. He's my hero. He's my god. And I thought you'd love him as much as . . ." She hesitated and lowered her head.

"As much as you do?" I asked.

She nodded and stared back at me, maybe searching for answers. It seemed like she was trying to look inside my soul, trying to figure out why Nikos wanted me. "Yes, Sabrina. I love Nikos. I love Nikos, and I'd do anything for him. But he doesn't belong to me. He never did, and he never will, although he'll always have a special place in my heart."

I looked deep into her eyes to understand her pain. "Does he know you love him? Why are you so sure he'll never love you?"

"He loves me, Sabrina, but he loves me like he would a sister. He's always treated me and respected me as such. And I'll never jeopardize what I have with him. He trusts me. I'll never betray him. I can't stand to see him sad. He deserves the best." She looked down at the ground again. "Do you love him, Sabrina? Do you love him for real?"

This woman worshiped the man I loved. But she sounded sincere, and I had to reveal my feelings to her even though it might upset her.

"Yes, I love him, Athena. I love him more than I've loved anyone in my life."

She sighed, put her glasses back on, and looked at me again. "Then promise me you won't hurt him. Promise me you'll make him happy and promise me you'll be patient with him. He'll open his heart to you. I'm sure he will. But if you break it, I'll never forgive you." She frowned and closed her eyes for a moment. "Nikos deserves to love, and I hope you are deserving of his love."

"I love Nikos, and all I want is to make him happy," I said.

We decided to get something to eat as it was close to two in the afternoon and we were both starving. After our argument, the mood between us lightened somewhat. During lunch, I asked Athena about Nikos's charity and the teens he was helping. She told me she managed the organization for him whenever he wasn't around. He loved the results it was yielding. Several teens had been accepted into the university already, and if it hadn't been for his help, those students would have dropped out of school by now.

Athena was as passionate about archaeology as Nikos was. I wondered why they hadn't clicked in a romantic way. And I realized I had no reason to be jealous of her and her intentions toward him. She'd convinced herself her infatuation with him would never materialize into a sexual relationship. She showed great respect for him and seemed to accept her status as his friend and coworker. She not only was protective of him but acted like his personal and emotional bodyguard. She seemed to have his best interests at heart, including accepting me as the woman he'd chosen to be with.

When we finished lunch, I asked her to drop me at the hotel. I wanted to rest. I needed to think about what was going on. I had to sort out my feelings regarding the mystery of Nikos's past and what I'd learned about him so far. I needed to be by myself. We agreed she'd come back later to take me to dinner.

I picked up my phone and lay down on the bed to rest my aching feet, which were sore from walking over the archaeological site's uneven terrain.

"Hi, my beautiful. How was your flight?" I heard Nikos's smoky, husky voice as he answered the phone.

"Hi, Nikos. The flight was smooth, but I miss you so much. I wish you were here with me. How are you?"

"I'll meet with Mr. Green later tonight. We have a business dinner."

"Have you seen Maggie?" I was apprehensive. We hadn't seen her or talked to her since she'd been in my hotel room a few nights ago. Her behavior was unpredictable, and I hoped she wouldn't embarrass Nikos in front of the guest.

"No. I'll see them at the restaurant. I don't know what she's planning or if she'll even mention anything about the museum sponsorship. I guess I'll find out this evening. Did you visit the site? How do you like Athena? Are you two getting along okay?"

"She's great. We visited the site earlier. It's wonderful to be here."

"I knew you were going to like it. What did she plan for the rest of the day?"

"She's planning to take me to dinner. I'm resting at the hotel now."

"Are you by yourself?" His tone was serious.

"Yes, I'm in my room. Why? I don't need a babysitter." I bit my tongue. I wanted to ask him about Santorini, but I shouldn't put Athena on the spot. Besides, it was better to ask him about it in person. I changed the subject before he could respond. "How is your mom doing?"

"She's doing fine, under the circumstances. I was with her this morning, and she's relieved to find out Yannis is in Athens, but she thinks what he's done is her fault. She's taking responsibility for his actions, and I must convince her not to. He's chosen the wrong path; there's nothing she could've done to prevent it. I hope she realizes it."

"Tell her I've been thinking about her."

"I'll do that, Sabrina. She likes you a lot. Are you comfortable in the hotel?"

"Yes, it's cozy and has a beautiful view. We have a small room."

"I don't need a lot of space to make love to you. We have all night tomorrow."

A huge smile sprouted across my face. I wanted this man and couldn't wait to be with him again. Everything I'd learned about him made me love him even more. Sooner or later, he'd have to tell me about his past. He needed to tell me who the woman in the picture was, what she meant to him, and what had happened in Santorini.

"Yes," I whispered. "We have all night tomorrow, and I can't wait to be in your arms. Have a good time tonight. I hope Maggie doesn't give you a hard time."

"I'm sure she won't be fool enough to bring our relationship into the picture, but I might be mistaken."

"She can be vicious, Nikos. But you can control the situation. Good luck." I blew him a silent kiss through the phone.

"Thanks. I'll give you a call tomorrow before I head to the airport. Have fun with Athena. I miss you."

"See you tomorrow. I miss you, too."

After I hung up, I searched for the only picture I had of him—the one from our weekend in San Antonio. I gazed at his handsome face, recalling the wonderful moments I'd spent with him. *I miss you, I love you, I need you, and I want to be with you for the rest of my life. Nikos, you're the best thing that's ever happened to me. Athena was right, I can never give up on you. I will never give up on you.*

Fifteen

I SAT IN THE lounging chair on the balcony of my room to appreciate the beautiful view of the Aegean Sea. I missed Nikos and couldn't wait for him to be there with me. I had no idea what would happen to our relationship once I got back to Houston, but I avoided thinking about it. I was way too involved with him now to leave, and I'd do whatever I had to to be with him, even if I had to relocate to Greece. It was intolerable to imagine it might be several months before I saw him again.

From the moment I'd arrived in Greece, I hadn't had time to be by myself and make sense of what had happened yet. I longed to be alone, to enjoy my solitude, to ponder my feelings and my life. I picked up the phone and dialed Athena.

"I'm sorry, Athena, but I'd rather stay in the hotel tonight. I'll have a bite to eat at the snack bar."

"Is there something wrong?" She sounded worried.

"No. I'm comfortable here, and I want to rest. I bet you have a lot of things to do, anyway. Thanks."

Athena sighed. "But Nikos asked me to—"

I didn't wait for her to finish. "Yes, Nikos asked you to make sure I'm okay. But I do want to be by myself tonight."

"Fine, I can't force you to go out. I'll come by tomorrow morning, and we'll go back to the site if you want. Nikos won't be here until late in the evening, and there will be very few archaeologists working on a Sunday."

"That's a plan. I'll see you tomorrow, then. Thank you for understanding."

"Kalinihta," Athena said before hanging up.

What a relief. At least I had the evening to myself. I wanted to rest and quiet my mind while looking out at the beautiful, calming sea. The week had brought a whirlwind of emotions not only for me but for Nikos as well. It had all happened too fast. I rewound the main events in my mind, including what I'd just found out about his life: there was some secret about his past and something which had happened in Santorini.

His mother had told me he'd loved once but he'd been hurt. She'd asked me to be patient. Athena had also asked me to be patient with him. Both of them loved him. Both of them knew what had happened to him. Both of them knew what had caused him to avoid commitment and serious relationships. And they both told me Nikos was in love with me. The woman in the picture must have had something to do with whatever happened in Santorini.

All this thinking had made me hungry, so I went down to the hotel coffee shop. After eating a falafel sandwich and drinking a cup of coffee, I crossed the street, heading to the beach. The sunset was coming soon, and I wanted to watch it. Greece was romantic and magical, and I needed this time to myself.

I laid the beach towel I'd brought from the hotel on the sand and sat on it, enjoying the wonderful view of the Aegean Sea. It reminded me of the sunset in Cape Sounion. My mind drifted back to that evening when Nikos made love to me at the Temple of Poseidon.

"How come such a beautiful woman is watching the sunset all alone?"

The question dissipated my dreamy memories as I looked up in surprise. Aleksy stood next to me holding two bottles of beer. His muscular physique and golden skin were accentuated by the white tank top he wore. His square jaw protruded forward, giving him a determined appearance. Aleksy was a handsome man. Before I could respond, he sat on the soft sand beside me.

"Please, have a drink with me." He offered me one of the bottles.

I hesitated before accepting it with a shrug. "Thank you. How did you find me here? I'm sorry; I wasn't expecting company." He had caught me utterly by surprise.

"I came by the hotel to say hi and the receptionist told me you'd gone for a walk. It was easy to find you. After all, this is a small town. Did you cancel your plans?"

"Cancel my plans?" I tilted my head.

"Athena said you already had plans for tonight when I invited you for dinner. Remember?" He took a sip of the beer, his eyes fixed on me.

"Oh, yes. I wanted to be by myself tonight," I said, hoping he would take the hint and leave. His sharp, piercing eyes made me uncomfortable. His proximity was intimidating.

"But I'm here now, so you don't need to be by yourself any longer." He smirked and winked at me. "You should never watch a sunset by yourself."

He draped his arm around my shoulder in a bold and direct move, and I stiffened.

"Aleksy", I said, removing his arm from my shoulder, "I'm seeing Nikos."

He tilted his head and frowned. "Are you serious? *Mr. Perfect* is seeing you? No wonder." His tone was sarcastic. It was clear he was jealous of Nikos.

I stared at him. "No wonder what? What do you mean?"

He drank his beer. "Don't get upset, sweetie. He's a lucky guy. No wonder he'd fall for a beautiful, intelligent, intriguing woman like you. Too bad I didn't meet you first. By the way, I'm going to be in Houston in two weeks."

I raised my eyebrows. "In Houston? Nikos didn't tell me one of his team members was going to Houston."

"I haven't told him yet. In fact, I haven't told anyone. I was offered a job as an associate professor of Classical Studies. It's for a faculty-in-residence position in one of the universities there. I accepted it. I plan on talking to Nikos before giving my notice."

He took another gulp of his beer.

"Well, congratulations. It should be a great opportunity for you. But why would you leave your job as a field archaeologist to teach?" I moved over a little to the side to keep some distance between us.

"The position I want here is already taken, sweetie. I don't think Nikos is leaving anytime soon." He grinned, winking at me again. Now I was certain there was a rivalry between the two of them. He gulped down the rest of the beer and set the bottle on the sand. "Change is good. And the way the economy is here in Greece right now, I don't see a big future. The government announced a desperate solution to keep the country afloat, and I'm bailing out at the right time."

"What desperate solution?" I took a sip of the beer. The cold liquid slid down my throat, refreshing me.

"You haven't caught up with the breaking news yet? The government closed all banks today. The European Central Bank froze the funding to our financial institutions. There was no choice but to shut down the system to keep the banks from collapsing."

"How bad is it?" I took another sip of the beer. If what Aleksy was saying was true, these measures would put a bigger strain on the financial support Nikos needed for the museum.

"Bad enough. Banks will close, and the stock market will shut down all week long. There'll be a daily sixty-euro limit on cash withdrawals from cash machines. It'll cause a lot of problems for us. I'm glad I transferred my money to an account in Houston in advance. Banking transactions to accounts outside Greece are prohibited for now."

I'd had no idea it was going to be this catastrophic for the Greeks. The country's financial system was crippled. The prospect of Greece being forced out of the euro was a reality. What Aleksy said was disturbing, and if Nikos hadn't been prepared for it, he wouldn't be able to leave Greece anytime soon.

"How long do you think this is going to last?" I placed my half-full beer bottle on the sand and rubbed my arms. A cool breeze blew as the sun set.

Aleksy shrugged. "Maybe a couple of months, but it's hard to say. When are you going back, sweetie?"

He was so close to me I could smell the beer on his breath. He'd probably been drinking before he came over.

"In a few days." The breeze got cooler, and I prepared to get up. Aleksy put his arms around me, locking me in place. His strong embrace brought instant warmth to my body as he sheltered me from the cooling air, but my muscles tensed. I dreaded the intimacy with him.

"You're cold, sweetie. I'll shelter you from the breeze while we watch the sunset."

I tried to get up, but he held me in place. "Aleksy, I want to leave. I want to go back to the hotel. I'm cold."

He tightened his embrace. "I'll keep you warm while you watch the sunset with me, sweetie. You're Nikos's girl, and I'll take good care of you while he's not here. Allow me to be a gentleman."

The sunset was nearly over, and I didn't want to argue with Aleksy. The sun was swallowed by the horizon and shades of orange and pink painted the darkening sky. My mind transported me back to Cape Sounion, where I had watched the same Aegean Sea as Nikos's protective arms surrounded me. Aleksy released me when the show was over and stood up at once, extending his hand to help me. I shook the sand off of my skirt and legs and picked up the towel and the bottle of beer, ready to go back to the hotel. As soon as I realized he was following me, I turned to face him.

"Aleksy, I'm going back to the hotel, and I want to be by myself," I said, hoping he'd leave me alone. "Thank you for the beer and the company."

He stared at me with a disquieting glow in his eyes as he frowned and shook his head. "Mr. Perfect is so lucky." He put his arms around my waist, pulled me close to him, and kissed me. I struggled out of his arms, and as soon as I was free, I smacked him on the cheek with my open hand.

A naughty smirk was stamped on his face. "You're a feisty beauty." He touched his cheek where I'd hit him. "I love women like you."

I gritted my teeth. "Stop it, Aleksy. Why are you doing this?"

His annoying expression didn't change; he seemed to mock me. "Because I'm tired of Mr. Perfect claiming it all to himself."

I crossed the street to the hotel, running from him. Aleksy's resentment toward Nikos seemed uncontrollable. Under the current situation, I didn't need to fuel someone's jealousy for Nikos. Aleksy soon caught up with me and grabbed me by the arm, but I yanked it out of his grip.

"Sweetie, I'm sorry. I didn't mean to disrespect you or Nikos. I think the few beers I had before coming here got to my head. Can we still be friends?" He extended his hand to me, and he narrowed his eyes as if he were expecting another blow from me.

I put my hands in my pockets to avoid touching him. I didn't want to be near him.

He lowered his gaze and drew his hand back, shoving it in his pocket. "Please, sweetie. I'll be in Houston soon, and I don't want to be on bad terms with you. Please. I shouldn't have gotten drunk." He bit his lip, waiting for me to say something. He sounded sincere, as if he regretted what he'd done moments ago.

"Stop calling me sweetie. You're making me uncomfortable, Aleksy."

He put his hands together in a pleading motion. "Please, Sabrina. I'm sorry. Give me a chance to start fresh with you in Houston, then. I promise you I'll behave. Forget what just happened."

I shook my head. "I don't know if I can do that. I don't trust you."

He released a loud sigh and threw his arms up in the air. "I messed up, okay? I messed up bad. Can I make up for it when I'm in Houston? Will you forgive me?"

"I won't promise you anything. When you're in Houston, it'll be another day, another time. We'll see." I took a step back, wanting to distance myself farther from him.

"Fair enough," he said. "No hard feelings, please? I'm sorry. I hope you won't tell anything about it to Nikos."

I sighed. "Good luck with your new job."

"I'll see you in Houston, then. Enjoy the rest of your stay in Greece if I don't see you again." He winked before walking away.

I rushed to my room and locked the door. All I wanted was to erase the feeling of his uncomfortable touch and his forced kiss. Aleksy's reaction had been a big surprise. Nikos elicited admiration from everyone who came into contact with him. I wasn't expecting to find someone who was this jealous of him, especially on his own team. Aleksy wanted Nikos's job, had called him Mr. Perfect, and had tried to seduce me. Could I ever trust him? I wasn't sure how I'd react if I ever saw Aleksy in Houston. I was sure he'd look me up, but I was determined to avoid him at all cost. I wouldn't forget how disrespectful he'd been toward me and Nikos. He was definitely not Nikos's friend. He was his rival, and after what had happened, I was more than suspicious of his intentions.

And although I was exhausted, sleep didn't come easily. It had been a challenging day for me, and my mind raced with thoughts of Nikos having dinner with Mr. Green and Maggie. I wondered how she'd treated him. Tomorrow couldn't come soon enough.

Sixteen

WHEN ATHENA ARRIVED AT the hotel in the morning, I was downstairs having breakfast at the coffee shop. The waitress had just brought me coffee and toast. Athena came to my table, bowed her head, and sat down across from me without saying a word. She looked sullen, and her lips formed a tight, straight line. After ordering a cup of coffee, she stared at me while fidgeting with the car keys still in her hands.

"Kalimera, Athena," I said in my broken Greek. "How are you? You look upset this morning." I took a bite of my toast and sipped the hot coffee, waiting for her to respond.

She cleared her throat but didn't say anything. Then she put the keys in the pocket of her jeans and ran her fingers through her beautiful long, curly hair. Her eyes emanated an accusatory gaze. The waitress placed the cup of coffee on the table in front of her and left. Athena picked it up, took a sip, and smacked her lips.

"I saw you and Aleksy on the beach last night. Was he the reason you wanted to be *'by yourself'*?" Her voice was full of venom.

I almost choked on the piece of toast I was chewing. I took a sip of coffee and stared at her in disbelief, my mouth dropping open once I'd stopped coughing. I shook my head.

"What were you doing? Spying on me?" I regained my composure at once, irritated by the petulance with which Athena had accused me. It was one thing for her to adore Nikos, but it was another for her to serve as his spy and watch my every move. I refused to think he'd given her instructions to follow me around. There was no motive for such an unreasonable action.

Her hands shook, and her heavy breathing made her nostrils flare up like a raging bull's. There I was, faced with another version of the Minotaur.

"No, I wasn't spying on you. I drove by the hotel because I wanted to make sure you didn't need anything. The receptionist pointed me in the direction of the beach."

I leaned back on the chair and crossed my arms over my chest. "And what did you see—Aleksy sheltering me from the cool breeze while we talked on the beach? That is exactly what happened."

She gaped at me. "And you think it's cool for you to snuggle with Aleksy on the beach watching the sunset while Nikos is in Athens? Aleksy is a big flirt. And he's always been Nikos's most fierce competitor. I can't believe you'd—"

I interrupted her. "You can't believe what, Athena? That Aleksy followed me to the beach while I was trying to have a moment to myself? I wasn't snuggling with him. I wanted nothing to do with him."

Athena took a sip of her coffee, watching me with an indifferent expression. She set the cup back on the table and lifted her hand to her lips. Her eyes stared at an invisible point behind me while she bit her nails and shook her head.

"It doesn't make any sense."

I didn't want to talk to her about what Aleksy did. I couldn't wait to see Nikos and tell him what had happened in Amphipolis so far. There was no reason for me to keep anything from him, including Aleksy's impending resignation, his new job in Houston, and his attempt to kiss me. Despite Nikos's hesitation to let me in, I wanted him to trust me. I had nothing to hide from him. Nothing. And I wasn't about to allow Athena to assume things she didn't know or get involved in my relationship.

"What doesn't make sense?" I asked.

"If you love Nikos so much, as you say, why would you allow another man to hug you at the beach while watching the sunset? What are your real intentions?" She stopped biting her nails and looked at her fingers for an instant. Then she picked up the coffee cup again and took another sip.

"Don't question my love for Nikos. I wasn't hugging Aleksy. I told him I'm seeing Nikos. He put his arms around me to protect me from the chilling breeze, that's all there was to it."

Athena sighed. "Whatever you say. I hope you don't break the heart Nikos is trying to mend."

"I love Nikos, and you know it. I'll never let him down. I'll never leave him." I finished my coffee. "Should we go to the site now?"

She nodded, called the waitress, paid for her coffee, and we walked in silence to her car. During the quick drive to the excavation site, I checked my cell phone for messages. Curt had sent me a text to tell me he'd already arrived, was missing me, and was happy to be home. There were also messages from Jane—she was curious about what was going on and why I hadn't come back with Curt. I'd forgotten to tell her I'd be in Greece for another week. As I hadn't communicated with her much since I'd left Houston, I sent her a quick reply, telling her I was visiting the tomb in Amphipolis and we'd catch up when I returned home.

There were only a few archaeologists working on the site, as Athena had mentioned. Excavations were not held on Sundays, but Amphipolis was an exception as they were still attempting to learn the significance of the discovery. I wanted to go inside the tomb by myself to see the large floor mosaic. By now, I was aware the chemistry between Athena and I had been tampered with. She didn't trust me after she saw Aleksy at the beach with me. No matter what I said, I had a feeling she'd always be suspicious of my intentions toward Nikos. Her love for him was hard to understand, but I had to accept her feelings. Nikos had great respect for her as a professional, and I was sure he'd get upset when he learned we hadn't gotten along the way he'd expected.

We walked through the stone arch and an open portal until we got to the headless and wingless Sphinxes. In front of the Sphinxes, there was a barrier wall of limestone blocks protecting the entry to the tomb. Large wooden timbers were installed to support the arch of the ceiling. Athena urged me to be careful while inside the tomb. We crossed to the second chamber, where the mosaic covered the entire floor.

She explained to me that the beautiful picture had been revealed not long ago. It was, in fact, a representation of the abduction of Persephone by Hades, as they'd suspected when it was found. The colorful mosaic was in white, black, gray, blue, red, and yellow. It showed a chariot pulled by two white horses and two male figures. The charioteer was Hades, a bearded man with a laurel wreath upon his head. Running ahead of the chariot was Hermes, the guide to the underworld. Persephone was shown with golden-red hair. She wore a white tunic with a thin red ribbon tied at her waist and a bracelet on her left wrist. Although the floor had a damaged area right in the middle, many of the loose pieces had been found, and they were working on its restoration. Beyond the mosaic floor, there was a doorway and threshold leading to a third chamber.

My phone buzzed as we admired the mosaic.

Nikos's voice greeted me. "Good morning, beautiful. How are you today?" I smiled as all the tension left my body. Hearing his voice had a calming yet exciting effect on me.

"I've been thinking about you the whole time," I said. "I'm inside the tomb with Athena right now. How are you? When are you getting here?"

He cleared his throat before continuing. "I don't know how to tell you this, but there's been another change of plans."

My body froze. What else could go wrong on this trip? I remained silent, waiting for him to continue.

"If you're done visiting the site, you can catch the next available flight and return to Athens."

"Why? What happened?"

Athena stared at me.

"The government has shut down the banks. Needless to say, the financial situation of the museum has been compromised even further. The museum director has ordered a mandatory meeting tomorrow morning to discuss the measures we must take to remain open during this difficult time. I'll have to leave Athena in charge of the operations in Amphipolis. They need me here. And I want you here with me."

I nodded in silence, thinking about what he'd just said. The situation was difficult. It was going to be even worse if Maggie went through with her threat to take her father's sponsorship away. Athena looked at me and raised her eyebrows.

"Yes, of course. I want to be with you too," I said. "I'll take the first plane back to Athens today."

"Is Athena next to you?"

I was looking at her. "Yes, she's right here. Do you need to talk to her?"

"If you don't mind. Send me the flight number as soon as you find out when you're coming back. I'm sorry our plans were all messed up."

I sighed. "It's not your fault. There was no way for us to have anticipated any of this. But I'm glad I'll see you later today. I miss you so much. Here's Athena."

I passed the phone to her. She grabbed it hurriedly and talked to Nikos in Greek. Their conversation was brief, and she soon hung up. "I'll get you to the airport at once." She gave the phone back to me.

She drove me to the hotel, and after I packed my duffle bag and checked out, we were on our way to the Kavala airport. We didn't talk much during the short trip. Athena was busy talking on the phone most of the time. When she wasn't, she apologized for being on the phone and speaking Greek. She explained she needed to get organized for the next day now that Nikos wasn't coming to take care of things.

I was glad I was going back to Athens. Aleksy came to my mind, and I trembled, remembering the uncomfortable sensation of his lips on mine. He wouldn't be able to talk to Nikos in person about his resignation. I wondered if he'd give his notice to Athena as she was now officially in command of the archaeological site.

When we got to the airport, she accompanied me to the airline counter and took care of the ticket change. My new flight was leaving in half an hour, and I'd be in Athens an hour later. I texted the information to Nikos right away.

"Do you want to grab something to eat before boarding?" Athena asked. "You don't have much time."

"I'm not hungry, thanks. You don't need to stay with me until I board. You're going to be busy this coming week, my flight is leaving soon, and you still have another hour on the road back to Amphipolis."

She shrugged. "Thanks for understanding. If you don't mind, I'm going."

I shook her hand. "Thank you so much for showing me around. I hope to see you again some other time."

"Yes, and maybe it will be a better time. Sabrina, I . . ." She hesitated while fidgeting with her car keys.

I raised my eyebrows, waiting for her to continue.

"I want to apologize for my jealousy. I don't want you to have a bad impression of me. I acted as if I were Cerberus guarding Hades's underworld." She sighed. "I'm sorry."

I wasn't expecting this from her. I frowned but couldn't help finding her comparison amusing. "Cerberus?" I chuckled. "Yes, you were safeguarding Nikos's ghosts and not letting anything out."

She shook her head. "I'm sorry. And I'm sorry for this morning and for doubting your integrity. Nikos is a god to me—untouchable, revered, admired. But when I saw you and Aleksy . . ." She paused and looked at me, as if searching for words. She lowered her head and looked away from me for a moment. Then she put the car keys in her pocket, crossed her arms, and stepped back.

"That's okay, Athena. I understand how you feel about Nikos. We should forget what happened and move on. No hard feelings. You don't need to apologize."

"No, you don't understand how I feel because it's not only about Nikos."

I cocked my head. "You and Aleksy?"

She nodded. "Yes. We've been seeing each other on and off. He's a big flirt, and he wants Nikos's position and all that Nikos has achieved. Our relationship doesn't get any easier. I'm Nikos's second-in-command with the team. But when I saw you and him at the beach . . ."

"Nothing happened at the beach, Athena. I'm not interested in Aleksy; believe me."

"I believe you. I was insane with jealousy because both Aleksy and Nikos seemed so into you." She uncrossed her arms, pulled the keys out of her pocket, and started fidgeting with them again.

I wanted to tell her Aleksy was going to quit and relocate to Houston. I wanted to tell her he'd kissed me. I wanted to tell her I didn't appreciate him and I didn't trust him. I wanted to tell her he was an ass. I swallowed hard. I couldn't do it. I couldn't hurt her feelings. I had no idea how deep her relationship with Aleksy was. But at this point, I had no intention of getting involved or helping to complicate it further.

"Have you thought maybe Aleksy was trying to make you jealous by getting closer to me?"

"I wish that was true. I'm not sure what's going on with us anymore."

The first call to board was announced, and it saved me from that awkward conversation.

"I guess you better get going," she said. "They're boarding now, and you still need to go through security."

I nodded. "Thank you again, Athena. Good luck. I'm sure you'll do a great job in Nikos's place. I wish you the best."

"Thank you for the vote of confidence. Have a nice trip back and enjoy the rest of your stay in Greece." She smiled faintly and left.

Kavala's airport wasn't big. I walked toward security, showed my passport and boarding pass, and was soon on my way to the gate. It was hard to believe that in such a short time I'd learned so much about Nikos and the people who worked with him. I had to digest all the information to understand the full picture. And more than anything, I wanted to tell Nikos my feelings and get him to open up and tell me all the secrets he'd been keeping from me.

Was he doing it to protect me? And if so, what was he protecting me from? Or was he doing it because he had no intentions of trusting me with his heart and his life? I needed to know. The rest of the week would be busy for Nikos. I'd have to take advantage of every minute I had with him. Once I got back to Houston, it would probably be a while before I saw him again. And Maggie could and certainly would inflict more damage upon an already precarious situation.

Seventeen

WHEN I LANDED IN Athens, I felt as relieved as if I were coming back home. As I approached the baggage claim area to meet Nikos, my heart nearly stopped when I spotted him. He stood in his god-like splendor looking at me with smoky, hungry eyes and embraced me with his strong arms before giving me a light kiss on the lips. His touch was enough to awaken the dormant desire within me. I wanted more of him.

"How is my goddess doing? You look tired. I'm sorry for all this mess."

"It would've been much better if you were there with me, but it was exciting to see the tomb nonetheless." My arms tightened around him, and I breathed in his irresistible scent. "The site is amazing. I'm glad I got to see it."

He planted another kiss on my lips, lingering a little longer than before.

"I can't wait to taste you. Let's get out of here." He took my duffle bag and led the way to the garage where his car was. Before opening the door for me, he pinned me to the car, and his mouth came down on mine with unquenchable hunger. I encircled his neck with my arms and immersed myself in his delicious, demanding kiss. My legs wobbled as I felt him getting harder against me. I would've loved to be taken by him right then and there. The warm moisture between my legs confirmed it. When he released me from his kiss, I was out of breath.

"I told you I couldn't wait to taste you," he said, grinning. "And I'll feast on you when we get home."

I held him tighter. "You have no idea how much I missed you, Nikos."

He kissed my head and opened the door of the car for me to get in.

"You don't need to go to the hotel, do you?" he asked as he drove through the airport parking garage.

"I need clean clothes."

"You won't need any clothes at my place." He chuckled. "I'll take you to the hotel in the morning on my way to the museum. If you want, you can check out and spend the rest of the week with me. Unless you prefer the view of the Acropolis from your window."

I gaped at him. "Are you serious?"

A big smile spread across my face. He was taking me to his place. I'd not only spend the night there, but I could spend the rest of the week with him as well. It would give me plenty of time to tell him what had happened in Amphipolis and discuss our future.

"It's up to you." He looked at me and winked.

"Yes, yes, I want to be with you. I'd love to!"

He rolled down the window and inserted his credit card to pay for the parking. When he finished the transaction, he reached for my hand, which rested on my leg, and caressed it.

"How was dinner with Mr. Green and Maggie?"

He sighed. "Not too good."

I waited to hear how their meeting had gone.

"She's unwilling to help the museum any longer, and she's blaming the economic situation. The banks are closed. There are restrictions on banking transactions to keep the financial system from collapsing. The government has imposed a daily limit of sixty euros on cash withdrawals from ATMs. It's going to be tough on all of us Greeks."

I caressed his hand. "What are you going to do?"

"I'm not sure yet. It's going to be a challenging week, that's for sure. Maggie said she's not willing to invest in a country with economic uncertainties as it may yield no returns for her. What a coincidence this happened right when she decided to stop sponsoring us. It made it easy for her to find an excuse." He shook his head.

"What about the money she brought from Houston to pay for the jewels' ransom?"

"She still has it. And she told Mr. Green she'll be investing it in the British Museum or other private collections in London." He released my hand and ran his nervous fingers through his hair. "This is a big mess."

I wanted to say something to soothe him, but nothing came to mind. I was worried about him. I was worried about how the cash withdrawal limits would affect him. And I was worried about his country's situation.

"How are you going to cope with it?"

He shrugged. "I have enough to get by for at least this week. It's going to be hard to continue with the excavations in Amphipolis. I won't be able to leave the country anytime soon if this goes on. And I have to help my mother. She can't live with the imposed limits on the cash withdrawals. By the way, I need to give her a call." He reached for his cell phone and speed-dialed a number, but there was no answer and he put it back in his shirt pocket. "She hasn't answered all afternoon. I'm starting to get worried."

"Why? What happened?"

"She visited Yannis in jail in the early afternoon and was supposed to meet her friends for coffee afterward. She called me after seeing Yannis, but I haven't heard from her since. I've already left her two messages. No answer, no call back yet. I hope she's having fun with her friends."

"She should be, right?" I tried to reassure him.

He nodded. "Sometimes, they decide to go to the movies, so I hope I'm not overreacting. She's been absentminded lately, even forgetting to turn her phone on."

I knew he worried about his mother, although he sounded calm and levelheaded. There'd been no break for him since he'd gotten back to Athens. Too much was going on. No wonder Aleksy called him Mr. Perfect. He always seemed in control of the situation, of his surroundings, and especially of his emotions. I wanted to talk to him about Athena and Aleksy, but it would have to wait. The least I could do was avoid bothering him with it.

When we got to his place, I noticed the picture of him with the woman was gone and there wasn't anything else in its place. The table's emptiness was blatant.

I followed him to his bedroom without mentioning it, grateful he'd been thoughtful enough to remove it from view.

"Here we are." He placed my duffle bag on his bed and came toward me, wrapping his strong arms around my waist. "You must be hungry and tired. Why don't you take a nice, warm bath while I cook something?"

"You're going to cook?" I raised my eyebrows while unbuttoning his shirt to run my fingers over his muscular chest. My attraction toward him drove me insane. I couldn't resist him whenever we were together, and I couldn't stop thinking about him whenever we were apart. The thought of going back to Houston and leaving him behind without knowing when I'd see him again slid into my mind like a treacherous viper. But I had to brush such thoughts aside and enjoy the time I still had left with him.

"Yes, I'm going to cook." His fingers found the hem of my shirt. He pulled it over my head and tossed it to the floor, moving next to unhook my bra. Then, he cupped my breasts with a soft touch while his fingers pinched my erect nipples. It turned the fountain within me up to full strength. Goosebumps formed all over my skin as I delighted in his lustful touch. His lips were soon on mine in a demanding kiss.

"Nikos," I mumbled against his lips. "I want you."

His hands slipped behind me, and his fingers trailed up and down my back, tickling me. I closed my eyes and moaned as my skin reacted to his soft and luscious touch. As I arched my back, his wet tongue licked one of my nipples before his teeth teased it with a light bite. My fingers clutched at his hair as his hardness pressed against my leg.

Suddenly, he released me. His breathing was hard, and his intense stare made me tremble. I was so ready for him I was about to beg him to take me.

"And I'm having you for dessert," he whispered.

I was panting. I should've known better. Of course he'd arouse me and then leave me yearning for more.

A naughty grin formed on his lips when I whimpered in frustration. "You should be patient."

"Why? I don't want to be patient. I want you. Now."

"I know you do." His fingers curled under my chin, lifting my face to his gaze. His stare was intense, and his tongue swiped across his upper lip as if he were ready to taste me. "And I want you. But I want you to want me with an insane, desperate desire. I want you to be so wet for me that I can make love to you all night long. I want to feast on you, Sabrina. I want to worship your body, and I want to please you until you can't take me any longer."

He hypnotized me. Even though every muscle and nerve of my body yearned for him, my head bobbed up and down, involuntarily agreeing to the torturous wait. He gave me a light kiss on the lips, and before I had the chance of saying anything, he left the room and closed the door behind him.

A loud sigh escaped, and I sat on the bed, feeling dizzy. The effect Nikos had on me was absurd. I thought it was impossible to want him more than I already did, but he was able to ignite a flame within me and make it burn with crazy, unrelenting desire.

After I took a shower, I left the bedroom dressed in one of his undershirts. It wasn't the provocative outfit I had envisioned wearing to have dinner with him, but under the circumstances, it would have to do. Nikos was on his cell phone, and when he saw me, he nodded with approval. He looked as attractive as ever wearing his jeans and no shirt, but his frown alerted me he was still worried. He put the phone on the counter and picked up a salad bowl.

"Were you able to reach your mom?" I asked.

"Not yet. Still no answer on her phone. I'm preparing Greek salad and spaghetti. It's not a fancy dinner, but I hope you enjoy it." He set the bowl on the table and continued cooking.

I followed him into the kitchen. "I'm sure I will. It smells delicious. Do you need any help?"

"No, princess, sit down and relax. I'll take care of it. You're my special guest."

I took my place at the table, admiring his perfect body and longing to touch him. Even though my adventure in Greece had been full of bumps and detours, I'd get to spend the rest of the week with him. This was better than I'd anticipated. I'd learn more about him and how he lived, and I was hoping to conquer him once and for all, which is all I wanted. I couldn't think about life without Nikos. My heart, my body, and my soul yearned for him. I knew I'd do anything for him. Anything.

He placed the dishes on the table, opened a bottle of red wine, and filled the glasses.

He raised his glass and bowed. "To my beautiful goddess."

I had never thought it was possible to be as happy as I was at this very moment, having a simple dinner. But it wasn't just a simple dinner; it was dinner cooked by the man I adored, for me, in his home. It was like living a dream.

"So, tell me about your trip. Did you have fun with Athena?" He served me some Greek salad.

"Yes." I fidgeted with a strand of my hair and looked down at my salad bowl, using the fork to play with an olive.

"No, you didn't. What happened? You two didn't get along?"

I had known he would see through me. I should've controlled myself better. I put the fork down and took a sip of the wine.

"Why would you say that? We had a great time. She's a wonderful person." I set the glass back on the table, picked up the fork again, and stabbed the olive with it.

"Sabrina, you can't hide your emotions from me. What happened between you and Athena?" He leaned forward and put his elbows on the table, setting his silverware aside.

What a stupid mistake on my part. There was no reason to bother him with my feelings toward Athena. I put the olive in my mouth and chewed. He glared at me, waiting for an answer.

"I was anxious, I guess, but there's nothing else to it. She was very helpful."

"Did you stay with her the whole time while you were at the excavation site?" His tone was serious, and his intensity intimidated me.

I sighed. "Nikos, that was one of the main problems I had with Athena. She was watching me, and it made me uncomfortable. It was as if she worried I was going to destroy or steal something. It was weird not being able to get out of her sight."

I wanted to ask him about Santorini. I bit my lip. I didn't want to betray Athena. But I was hoping he'd tell me what bothered him about me visiting the site on my own.

He took a sip of his wine. "The excavation site is dangerous, Sabrina. You're not used to working around risky outdoor digging areas. I wanted to make sure you didn't wander into an unsafe area. Athena knows the place well, and she's the only one I'd trust with your safety while I wasn't there." He set his glass back on the table.

I closed my eyes for a second, remembering when Athena had told me she didn't even know why he'd allowed me to go to Amphipolis after what had happened in Santorini. Why wasn't he going to say anything about it? I played with my salad again and stabbed a piece of feta cheese. "Well, to tell you the truth, it was embarrassing not being able to explore the site on my own, especially when I realized Athena was kind of . . . evaluating me."

He narrowed his eyes as he leaned back in the chair. "Evaluating you? What do you mean?" His fingers curled under his big hands, and he rested his fists on the table.

I knew I was opening a can of worms. I had to tell him what had happened; there was no escaping it. I'd told myself back in Amphipolis I had nothing to hide from Nikos. And it's how I wanted my relationship with him to be.

"She was studying me to see if I was fit to be with you because she loves you." I swallowed the piece of cheese.

"I think you're jealous, but you don't have to be. Athena doesn't love me. She's in love with Aleksy, another one of my team members.

You didn't meet him?" He chuckled, picked up his fork and knife and started working on his salad.

The blood rushed to my face as I remembered Aleksy's unwelcome kiss and how I had disliked it. The whole experience had been disturbing. I shook my head, picked up the glass of wine and took another sip. My mouth was dry. "Yes, I met him. But I don't think they're seeing each other. Aleksy isn't interested in Athena." I bit my lip.

He raised his eyebrows but kept working on his salad. "How do you know that?"

How I regretted having initiated this conversation. I wanted to tell Nikos about Aleksy's advances toward me and his impending resignation from the archaeological team. And about his upcoming move to Houston. But I wasn't sure if this was the right time to talk about it. I picked up my glass and drank the rest of the wine in one gulp.

"There's something I need to tell you."

He leaned back again and rested his silverware on the table. "I'm all ears. Tell me. What happened in Amphipolis?" He frowned as he crossed his arms over his chest.

My body was tense. I held the empty glass and took my eyes off him to glance at the side table where his picture with the woman had been a few days ago.

"I had no idea what to expect in Amphipolis by myself. Things are happening so fast, Nikos. And I still don't—"

The unexpected buzz of his cell phone interrupted me. He put his napkin on the table and rushed to grab the phone from where he'd left it on the kitchen counter. I sighed. At least the distraction would give me a few minutes to dissipate my anxiety.

Nikos answered the phone and came back toward the living room. Before he could reach the table, he froze, staring at me with blank, glassy eyes. The color left his face, and he was as white as a ghost. I'd never seen him like this before. He looked fragile, scared, breathing as if the air wasn't reaching his lungs. He ran his fingers through his hair while the color returned to his face little by little. When he spoke to the person on the phone, his voice was shaky and hardly audible. I had no idea what he was saying, but I sensed something terrible must've happened.

The conversation didn't last long. He lowered the phone from his ear as if in slow motion, staring at it in disbelief, as if in a trance. I wanted to run to him and hold him in my arms, but I was too scared to move or say anything. After a few seconds that seemed like an eternity, he took his place back at the table. He clutched the phone with shaking hands, looked at me, and cleared his throat.

"They took my mother."

My eyes popped out of my head. "What? Who?"

He shook his head. "I knew something wasn't right. They think it was Yannis's fault. They didn't get the ransom money for the jewels, and they have my mother now."

I covered my mouth with my hand.

"I have to call the Interpol agents. I have to get her, I have to . . ." His voice trailed away. He stood up and paced around the table. "I can't secure that much money in only a few days. It's a lot of money and the banks won't allow it . . ." His hand curled into a fist, and he slammed it against the wall next to him. One of the hanging pictures fell with a loud bang and crashed to the floor. The glass frame shattered into a million little pieces. He dialed a number on his cell phone and had a brief exchange of words in Greek. When he finished talking, he looked at me and took a deep breath.

"I'm sorry." He shook his head. "I have to go to the Interpol office and discuss what to do to save my mother."

I got up and approached him. It was hard to imagine how frightening the situation was for him. One more thing on his plate, and this time it had to do with the person he loved and respected the most. I wanted to ask him more about Ms. Soulis's kidnapping, but I knew now was not the time.

I wrapped my arms around him. "What are you going to do?"

His strong, firm arms enveloped me in return. "I'm not sure, my princess. I don't have that kind of money, and even if I did, the banks wouldn't allow me to withdraw it now. I have to talk to the agents. See what they found out about the kidnappers. Negotiate, maybe. All I know is I must get my mother back as soon as possible."

"What if we talked to Dr. Jones, or asked Mr. Wallendorf to help out?" I suggested, out of better ideas.

"No. This has nothing to do with Mr. Wallendorf. I don't know all the details of my brother's involvement in the heist yet, but this seems to be a personal attack against him."

"But your mother was taken because of the jewels. Whether it's a personal attack on Yannis or not, the reason you're involved in this situation is because of Mr. Wallendorf. He helped facilitate lending the jewels to his friend's private collection. He could help."

Nikos shook his head. "No. Maggie isn't willing to sponsor the museum any longer. I don't need to drag her and her father into my personal life. I'll have to figure something out."

I sighed and tightened my embrace. "What can I do to help you?"

He kissed my head. "What do you want to do? You should be enjoying yourself instead of being involved in my mess. I'm sorry."

"Take me to the hotel."

He raised his eyebrows. "Are you sure?"

"Yes." I rested my head on his shoulder. "I don't want you to worry about me. You need to take care of the situation. I'll be fine there."

"That's true. I'll feel better if you're at the hotel, moving around the city more easily and entertaining yourself while I'm dealing with this." He caressed my hair.

"Do what you need to do to save your mom. Don't worry about me." I left and got dressed as fast as I could. When I came back to the living room with my duffle bag, he was waiting with the keys in his hand.

We drove to the hotel in silence. Nikos seemed to be in deep thought. I was sure his mind was cloudy and confused with the awful news. Members of a criminal organization had kidnapped his mother. I was certain he was making a huge effort to make sense of it and be levelheaded.

He parked in front of the hotel and got out of the car. The

parking attendant opened the door for me, and I hopped out. Nikos came around to say goodbye.

He looked at me with sad, droopy eyes. "I have no idea what's going to happen from now on until I get my mother back."

I touched his face with the tips of my fingers, caressing him with love. "Don't worry about me. Do what you have to do. You've done a lot for me already. You'll find a way to get your mom to safety, and if I can help in any way . . . please allow me to."

He reached for my hand and brought it to his lips. His soft, quick kiss made me tremble. "Thank you. These have been some of the worst weeks of my life. You're the only good thing that has come out of it, and I'm not even able to enjoy being with you."

"Nikos . . . please be careful."

He gave me a quick kiss on the lips before directing his attention to the hotel employee.

"Take good care of her for me. If she needs anything, contact the manager and tell him she's my special guest."

The man nodded, took my duffle bag from Nikos, and opened the door so I could enter the lobby. Nikos released my hand and was gone in a heartbeat. Thickness filled my throat.

Back in the familiarity of my room, I stepped onto the balcony to look at the beautiful Acropolis in front of me. Although the older Acropolis was burned by the Persians, the monument standing now, built by Pericles, symbolized the glory of the Golden Age of Athens. The drama of the Greeks now shaped the background of my own real life, but I was far from having a glorious ending.

I came to Athens looking forward to a wonderful, tantalizing week with the god of my dreams. I had hoped to get to know him better and become part of his life, and I was now left with more questions than before. What was going to happen? How would he be able to save his mother? What could I do to help him?

I had no answers, and the uncertainty made me panic. Nikos didn't have the money to pay the kidnappers. His mother's life was in jeopardy. I was so powerless. I wanted to do something for him, but what? I had to do something, though. I couldn't just sit and wait and despair.

Eighteen

MAGGIE ANSWERED HER DOOR dressed in a hotel bathrobe. She had a towel wrapped around her head. Steam fogged her room.

"What are you doing here? It's late, and I'm getting ready to go to bed." Her tone was cold as ice.

"I need to talk to you. Please. It won't take long." My heart was beating fast, and my hands were shaking.

She reluctantly allowed me to come in after scanning me from head to toe.

"If you're going to ask me to reinstate the sponsorship of the museum, you're wasting your time," Maggie said, placing her hands on her hips and tapping her foot on the floor.

"Nikos needs help, Maggie. His mother was kidnapped by the same guys who stole the jewels. It's a complicated issue, but the bottom line is they want the ransom money," I said without blinking.

Maggie frowned, and her lips formed a straight line. She walked toward the bed and sat down, removing the towel from her head and rubbing her hair with it.

"You expect me to give Nikos the money to save his mother? Did he ask you to come here? Why didn't he come instead of you? Where is he?"

I kneeled down on the soft carpet opposite her and stared into her

146

eyes. "No, he didn't ask me to come here. He has no idea I'm here, and he won't ask you to help him. He's at the police station talking to the detectives. And yes, I expect you to save his mother. You have the ransom money, and if you were willing to use it to save the jewels, I expect you to use it to save someone's life. Nikos's mother's life."

She tossed the towel aside, grabbed a comb sitting on the bedside table, and started combing her towel-dried hair.

"Why would I do this for Nikos? He humiliated me in front of you. I've no reason to help him."

"Maggie, for God's sake!" I stood and threw my arms up in the air. "You can't be so heartless. He needs your help. Forget about that incident. Please. What can I do? How can I convince you to help him?"

A sly smirk formed on her lips, her hands never pausing as she continued combing her hair. "What are you willing to do for him?"

"Anything!" I yelled. "I'll do anything for Nikos. You have no idea how much this is affecting him. I can't stand to see him suffering so much. But I don't have the money. Even if I could get help from home, with Greece's current economic situation the banks won't allow a transfer this big and—"

"Even leave him?"

"What?" I asked, puzzled by her interruption.

She tossed the comb to the side of the bed. "Would you do anything for Nikos, including leave him?"

"L-leave him?" I stuttered.

"Yes, you heard me right. If I agree to pay for his mother's release, I want something in return. I want him. He was mine before you stole him from me. I want you out of the picture. I want you gone from his life."

My legs gave out, and I fell to my knees on the floor. My body was shaking. I gaped at Maggie in disbelief. I wasn't expecting this blow. How could I leave Nikos? The thought had never crossed my mind when I came to ask her for help. I'd been so naïve to think she'd offer her help willingly.

"Maggie, please. Be reasonable." My voice faltered.

Her eyes radiated a coldness I'd never seen before. Maggie was determined to get what she wanted, no matter how. And because I came asking for her help, I'd given her a way to get back into the game with Nikos. What was I doing?

"You're the one who needs to be reasonable, Sabrina. Did you ever think you had a chance with Nikos? You don't deserve him. You can do nothing for him. Look at you. All you can do is come to me for help. You can't save his mother, you can't save his museum, and you can't save him. Without my help, he's ruined. And you'll be the cause of his ruin if you don't realize this and get out of my way." She picked up the towel again and tapped it lightly against the ends of her long blonde hair.

My vision blurred from the sudden tears trickling down my cheeks. Although I hated what she said, Maggie had a point. I could do nothing to help Nikos. I had no money, no power, no influence. The only thing I had to offer him was my unconditional love, but that's not what he needed. He needed someone strong beside him. He needed someone who could help him save his mother, save his museum, and save his job.

I wasn't that person. Maggie was right. My pulse was weakening, and my head throbbed. I took a deep breath to bring air back into my lungs. I didn't want to collapse in front of her.

I nodded and lowered my head in resignation, trying to hide my tears. "What do you want me to do? Nikos doesn't know I'm here. He can't know I came here to ask you for help."

She got up and walked toward the balcony, opening the door to look at the beautiful view outside. I remained where I was. I had no strength left. The thought of leaving Nikos and not seeing him, kissing him, or touching him ever again was devastating. I was ready to sacrifice for love, but it never occurred to me I'd have to leave the man I loved like this. There was no backing out now. I had to help him save his mother.

This is the only way, I tried to convince myself.

"First, you need to go back to Houston. No later than tomorrow. There's nothing else for you to do in Greece. I'll get you a new one-way ticket. That way, you don't have to mess with change fees and overbooked seats because this is a last-minute trip."

Before I could say anything, she pulled out her cell phone and speed-dialed a number.

"Maggie here. I need you to book a flight from Athens to Houston for tomorrow." She paused to listen to the person she'd called. "I don't care what class or what airline; get the first available seat out of Athens. I'll text you the name of the passenger." She hung up and sent a text. "Done. My dad's secretary is super efficient. I'll tell you the flight you'll be on as soon as she sends me the details."

"How do I know you'll honor your part of the deal? How will you offer the money to Nikos? No one knows about the situation but me. I can't leave until Ms. Soulis is safe."

Maggie stepped back into the room and sat on the bed close to where I knelt without moving. I rubbed my face with the back of my hands to dry the insistent tears.

"Don't be ridiculous. I want Nikos, and this is my chance to get him back. I won't pass this opportunity up, but I need to make sure you're not around. I don't want him distracted by your presence. I'd have to call him anyway because Green wants him around when we take the jewels to London on Tuesday. But the whole plan will have to change now."

I cleared my throat. "What are you going to do?"

"I'll call him right now." She began to dial his number.

"No . . ." I mumbled. I hated the fact that she'd talk to him.

"You want me to save his mother or not? Make up your mind."

A lump in my throat obstructed my voice, but I nodded and managed to mutter, "Go ahead." I clutched my hands together in a tight grip.

She dialed his number. My heart was about to stop beating. I didn't want him to answer. I didn't want him to tell her anything. I didn't want him to accept her help. What had I done? He'd have to accept her help. It was the only way to save his mother.

"Hello, Nikos. It's me, Maggie. I know it's late, and I apologize for calling you at this time. But I need to finish the plans to travel with the jewels to London on Tuesday, and Green wants you to be there." She paused, waiting for him to say something. "Yes, of course I'm aware it's a last-minute request, but it's what Green suggested this afternoon. He feels much more comfortable with you around." She paused again. I wished I could hear what Nikos was saying. "Sorry, but I must confirm this now. If you can't be there, Green will change the flight. I can't deal with this any longer. I've had enough of these damned jewels."

I realized Maggie was pressuring Nikos into telling her about the situation with his mom. He wouldn't be able to attend to Mr. Green's request, and he wouldn't lie.

"Nikos, I can't wait. I need an answer now. The scheduled flight is Tuesday. Won't you be at the museum anyway?"

She kept pushing him. I closed my eyes and rubbed my forehead.

"You don't know? Why? You sound agitated, darling. What's going on?"

I bit my lip, waiting for her next words. I was about to explode inside. I needed to listen to what Nikos was saying.

"Oh, my God, are you serious? When did this happen? Where are you? Why didn't you call me?"

There. She'd won. He'd told her. Now the game was on for sure, and I was miserable for it. I'd set him up for Maggie. I'd betrayed my love for him. But it was the only viable solution, wasn't it? Maggie was the only one who could help him. I'd never forgive myself if something happened to his mother and I'd done nothing to save her. Even if it meant leaving him. The ultimate sacrifice. Had I acted prematurely? Maybe I should've waited to see what the detectives recommended before acting on impulse. But it was too late now. What had I done?

I could taste his lips. I could smell his irresistible, fresh scent. My body trembled. I was numb. I'd lost Nikos.

"I'll come over right away. I should talk to the investigators. I still have the money for the ransom of the jewels. We'll get your mom back in a heartbeat."

She was quick. I wondered if he'd even think twice about her offer. It was his mother, after all.

The ghost of his touch caressed my skin.

"What do you mean you don't need my help? I don't think you have the luxury of rejecting my offer. This is a serious situation, Nikos. I'd never forgive myself if something happened to your mom when I have the money to save her. I want to come over so I can talk to you and the investigators. I'll be there shortly."

What had I done? I had opened Pandora's box and lost the man of my life.

Maggie hung up and shrugged. "There. He told me. You're not involved whatsoever. And we're done. I'm going to the Interpol office now to take care of it. And Nikos will be mine again, at last. This has been the best deal I've made in a long time, Sabrina. Thank you. I was losing hope with Nikos."

"Don't be sarcastic, Maggie. This has never been a game to me. I love Nikos, and I'll always love him, no matter what." I stared at her with a blank expression. How dare she say that? Did she realize how much it hurt me to leave Nikos? It was all a game to her. Win or lose. She didn't care about anyone's emotions or feelings. She was only interested in getting her way.

The thickness in my throat was choking me. I felt nauseous. I wanted to throw up. It disgusted me that I'd accepted this deal. I hated myself for having allowed Maggie to force her way into Nikos's life again. My world was over. How could I live without Nikos? I had promised his mother I would make him happy. I had promised Athena I'd never leave him.

"There's nothing else for us to talk about. You can go now. I'll send you the flight information soon. Go pack and have a great trip to Houston tomorrow."

I stood up as if in a trance, balancing on my wobbly legs so I wouldn't fall. I was weak, feverish, and sick. I was dead inside, and my heart was broken beyond repair.

I could feel his strong arms embracing me. *My Nikos, my god, my man, my dream. How can I leave you? How can I go on without you? Forgive me, my love. Forgive me. I'm doing what I think is best for you.*

"You shouldn't contact him anymore. Don't call him again. And one more thing, Sabrina." Maggie opened the door for me to leave. "Nikos can never, ever find out about our deal."

"He won't," I said in a numb voice, and I left the room.

To Be Continued

In

Olympian Love

About the Author

Andrya Bailey is an award-winning contemporary romance writer who lives in Texas, USA. She enjoys traveling and visiting museums and historical landmarks, where she can learn about art and history, both of which she usually incorporates into her stories. She loves to write love stories with strong alpha males and exotic scenarios—after all, what better fantasy is there?

Olympian Passion, the first book of the Olympian Love series, is the recipient of a 5-star seal from Readers' Favorite and is the 2016 New Apple e-book Contemporary Romance—Solo Medalist winner.

Follow her on Facebook:
   https://www.facebook.com/andryabailey

Follow her on Twitter: @AndyB0810

We hope you enjoyed reading *Olympian Heartbreak*. We'd sincerely appreciate it if you could leave a review on the site where you purchased it from. Thank you!

www.ingramcontent.com/pod-product-compliance
Lightning Source LLC
Chambersburg PA
CBHW032015170626
46807CB00006B/2815